International Praise for An

NOMINATED FOR THE 201(
AND BEST TRANSLA

ONE OF *Flavorwire*'S TOP 50 IND

ONE OF *Entropy M*

ONE OF *B*
TRA

INCLU
31 WOM

"Anne Garréta's *Sphinx*, an O
gender—a feat that's all the more impressive in French, which has gender baked into its grammatical constructs." —DAN PIEPENBRING, *The Paris Review*

"Merciless and androgynous, this sphinx-like love soon renders gender stigmas pointless." —CHARLOTTE GROULT, *The Paris Review* staff pick

"[Garréta has] been called influential and groundbreaking, and with this, her first translation into English, it is easy to see why. *Sphinx* is an important contribution to queer literature—fascinating, intelligent, and very welcome." —SARA RAUCH, *Lambda Literary*

"The set-up is such a classic, relatable tale of falling in—and out—of love that one wonders why gender has always been such a huge factor in how we discuss relationships, in fiction and otherwise….So, the author, and the translator, created their own language, championing love and desire over power and difference." —MADDIE CRUM, *Huffington Post*

"A short but deep exploration of the nature and complexity of desire and longing." —*Publishers Weekly*

"A master of thought and language, an astounding authority and elegance." —ANNE SERRE, *Marie Claire*

"Garréta finds endless shades of in between and out of bounds, her characters taking shapes no other text before—or since—has imagined." —LAUREN ELKIN, *Bookforum*

"A unique novel, *Sphinx* succeeds in telling a love story without names or genders, allowing the reader to interpret the novel however they wish. Set in Paris and calling to mind the work of James Baldwin, this both feminist and LGBT book is deeply evocative in its word usage as it celebrates love without the constraints of gender." —*World Literature Today*

"A powerfully compelling narrative." —TOBIAS CARROLL, *Vol. 1 Brooklyn*

"Garréta's mastery is in never committing to one allusion or formation, like the mythological sphinx. Subsequently, she avoids didacticism, while still hinting at moral and philosophical dilemmas." —SARAH COOLIDGE, *ZYZZYVA*

"The strength of [*Sphinx*] lies in its philosophical eloquence…Take away gender and race from the book, and what's left? Love, viewed as a nihilistic transcendence… considerably more than a language game." —ADAM MARS-JONES, *London Review of Books*

"Quite remarkable, and a rewarding piece of experimental—in the best senses of the word—fiction." —MICHAEL ORTHOFER, *Complete Review*

"Centering her tale on the love and lust of a young couple in the Parisian underworld allows Garréta to train our eyes on the physical beauty of youth, the sensuality of anonymous bodies, and our preconceptions regarding both." —JANE YONG KIM, *Words Without Borders*

"The trajectory and style of the writing are breathtaking, and…Emma Ramadan's translation is superb." — TOM ROBERGE, Albertine Books

"By removing gender from language, the author forges a language that stands at a remove from daily discourse as we know it; these stylistic efforts have been made in order to force us to scrutinize the ways we perceive each other in new ways." —JOHN TAYLOR, *The Arts Fuse*

"Garréta's removal of gendered grammar is less an indictment of gender—or sign-bearing bodies—and more of a narrative challenge, a queering of language. This is also to say *Sphinx* is less of a queer romance novel than it is a poetic queering of love itself." —MEGHAN LAMB, *The Collagist*

"The fragments that do surface from this unconscious reservoir are vividly and eloquently incarnated. This is particularly true of the prose around lights, music, and bodies—the primary elements that compose nightclubs. They are rendered in rapturous tones…I could go on—exquisite fragments like these are packaged in nearly every page." —JOHN TAYLOR, *The Rumpus*

"…a bold, strange, perfectly constructed novel." — EVA DOMENEGHINI

"A literary feat…The most beautiful praise one can give to a novel is to say that it is unlike anything else…What she has done is a kind of masterpiece." —JACQUES LAURENT

"Astonishing." —SYLVIE GENEVOIX, *Madame Figaro*

"A remarkable entrance into the literary scene… A first novel so promising that it foreshadows, one hopes, a long literary career." —JOYSANE SAVIGNEAU, *Le Monde*

"Anne Garréta has achieved what is certainly the most difficult and rarest feat in a first novel-memoire: she disconcerts the reader."—ANDRÉ BRINCOURT, *Le Figaro*

"The sharpest analyses of intelligence and of the heart… A celebration of the most beautiful and most fragile of bodies, of all endangered flesh, destined to die." —GEORGES ANEX, *Le Journal de Genève*

NOT ONE DAY

—

Anne Garréta

TRANSLATED FROM THE FRENCH BY
EMMA RAMADAN AND THE AUTHOR

DEEP VELLUM PUBLISHING

DALLAS, TEXAS

Deep Vellum Publishing
3000 Commerce St., Dallas, Texas 75226
deepvellum.org · @deepvellum

Deep Vellum Publishing is a 501c3
nonprofit literary arts organization founded in 2013.

Copyright © Éditions Grasset & Fasquelle, 2002
Originally published in French as *Pas un jour* by Anne F. Garréta,
Editions Grasset & Fasquelle in Paris, 2002
English translation copyright © 2017 by Emma Ramadan
First edition, 2017

ISBN: 978-1-941920-54-1 (paperback) · 978-1-941920-55-8 (ebook)
LIBRARY OF CONGRESS CONTROL NUMBER: 2016959431

—

Cet ouvrage a bénéficié du soutien des Programmes d'aide à la publication de l'Institut Français.
This work, published as part of a program of aid for publication,
received support from the Institut Français.

—

Cover design & typesetting by Anna Zylicz · annazylicz.com

Text set in Bembo, a typeface modeled on typefaces cut by Francesco Griffo
for Aldo Manuzio's printing of *De Aetna* in 1495 in Venice.

Distributed by Consortium Book Sales & Distribution · (800) 283-3572 · cbsd.com

Printed in the United States of America on acid-free paper.

Table of Contents

or perfected our corruption: "We must have spectacles in the great cities of the post-modern era, and confessions for idolatrous people. I have seen the mores of my times, and I have published these stories.

Would that I had lived in an age when I should have thrown them into the fire!"

The irony delights you before you've even written a line. You will play at a very old game that has become the hobbyhorse of a modernity balking at radical disenchantment: confession, or how to scrape the bottoms of mirrors.

On a September day in 1835, strolling near Lake Albano, a man named Stendhal or Henri Beyle or Henri Brulard—which is it? Who knows... perhaps all three—draws in the sand the initials of the women he has loved: V, An, Ad, M, Mi, Al, Aine, Apg, Mde, C, G, Aur, and finally Mme Azur. The first name of this last one escapes him. The list of an unlucky Don Juan: "In reality, I had only six of the women I have loved."

Here H.B. is tempting you with the outline of a project both melancholy and tinged with cruel irony, and perfectly suited to your convalescence: the stammering alphabet of desire.

If you aim to thwart your habits and inclinations, you might as well go about it systematically. Here's what you have resolved to do (there's no more radical way to differ or dissemble from oneself than what you're planning here). It comes down to a single maxim: Not one day without a woman.

Which simply means that you will allocate five hours (the time it takes a moderately well-trained subject to compose a standard academic essay) each day, for a month, at your computer, aiming to recount the memory you have of one woman or another whom you have desired or who has desired you. That will be the narrative: the unwinding of memory in the strict framework of a given moment.

You will write as one goes to the office; you will be the archivist of your desires, thirty-five hours a week. Five hours per initial, no more, no less.

You will take them in the order in which they come to mind. You will then put them down, neutrally, in alphabetic order. To hell with chronology.

You will refrain from using your customary instruments: no pen, nothing but the keyboard (to the last syllable of recorded time). No draft, no notebook to gather bits and pieces, no considered and composed architecture, no rules other than the purely material and logistical ones that you've already assigned to the act.

No other principle than to write from memory. You will not try to capture things as they happened, nor will you reconstruct them as they might have happened, or as you might have liked them to happen. You will tell them as they appear to you at the precise moment you recall them.

Stabbing at your keyboard, you will decimate your memories. And who cares if at the end of your five hours of recollection, nothing will have been consummated? Who cares whether we've actually had the women we've desired? Writing at the whim of memory twists and turns on uncertainty. Like desire itself, never assured of its end or its object.

No erasures, no rewrites. Sentences as they come, without plotting them, cut off as soon as they're left hanging. Syntax matching composition.

Perhaps you will finally manage, in some feeble way, to emulate your peers, who recount their every experience, spewing out volumes of life matter—and buy into it.

It would have been better had you kept a journal. But you do not possess the talent of your peers. From day to day, you would have had nothing to report: nothing ever happens to you except in remembering. You only grasp the moment in distant memory, once oblivion has given things, beings, events, the density that they never have in the broad evanescence of daylight.

Your days are made of vapor, of imperceptible condensation. The world (and you with it) is a phantom that only time, the sands of time, makes visible and in the same moment erases. In full daylight, they don't even cast a shadow. An exquisite sensitivity, a photographic plate slowly revealing the image. But there seems to be no fixer for it: exposed to the light of the screen, of the page, and held too long under our gaze, memory dissolves without remission, leaving behind only the image of an image, a snapshot taken at the moment of recollection. From copy to copy of remembrance, it fades, moves. Soon nothing remains but the caricature—and the few details that the gaze has selectively magnified.

In one fell swoop, you will focus and dissipate yourself through thought. You will give yourself over, at set hours, to a purely discursive mental libertinage, you who have long ago renounced libertinage, and have adopted a simplicity of morals that would amaze your peers. And that you certainly never would have been able to imagine when you believed that you were only living in the present.

You will dissipate yourself through thought, in order to dispel the desires that you might still feel, that you are liable to feel even though you have learned to thwart their most trivial ploys.

Let's say it's a beautiful summer night, that after three months spent lounging on your sofa waiting for the double fracture in your right leg to heal, which left you with two metal plates, thirteen screws, and the leisure to analyze the subtle nuances of physical pain accompanied by the taste of morphine mixed with grenadine, to marvel at your luck, all things considered, in getting off so lightly after that absurd accident. For when you developed the memory of it, you finally saw that it could have cost you your life or your body, cut in half by the force of a relatively serious paralysis, that after these three months and a new lease on life, on movement, it's a truly beautiful summer night, a night when the body, free at last from too much pain, rediscovers all of its appetites helter-skelter: for dancing, for other bodies, for women. It's a perfect evening for sitting on the terrace of a café, watching the women go by. Desire would surely come hurtling down its slope, natural and abrupt, and before even realizing it you would probably have accrued additional memories.

In this regard, desire and pain are alike—your accident taught you this. Only when they take you by surprise do they get out of hand. You wake up after a respite and they will overwhelm you. To keep them in check requires a cool head, focus and consistency.

To dissipate, evade, or sidetrack your desires, such is the purpose of this little experiment you are attempting and which you hope will suffice to keep you going until you board the plane that will carry you across the Atlantic to the other coast of desire. Or to put it another way, you who were frivolous for so long, a fact the stories that you intend to unwind each day of this month of July 2000 will fully illustrate; you who were frivolous for so long, and you whose natural, and certainly human, tendency (exacerbated by all the typically French fondness for fickleness which confounds grace and flippancy, pleasures of flesh and vanity) is far from tamed. For a long time now, you've resolved to stop living as a slave of your disorderly desires.

For life is too short to resign ourselves to reading poorly written books and sleeping with women we don't love.

B*

Memory of a body: inscribed in a given space, anchored in light.

Seated, legs stretched before you, in an armchair like those Balthus wrapped in the ruffled fabric that haunts his paintings, in the orb of light of one of those rusted iron floor lamps imagined by the same Balthus, a bottle of cognac propped up against your stomach. To your right, the glass-top table overloaded with papers, books, two computers. To your left, the dinner table (a plank set on two massive trestles borrowed from an artist's studio), not yet cleared.

Behind you, a ledge on the white-washed wall which serves as a shelf for still more books. Facing you, the staircase slanting up to the mezzanine and your bed. Now and then you open the bottle of cognac to refill your glass, and you reflect.

A little while ago, you walked your guests home. Who were they? You remember only *** (who was your lover, and present at all of your dinner parties) and B*, who had come to give a talk in this Roman villa where you spend your nights reading, strolling through the gardens, playing pool alone in the deserted bar.

No memory of the dinner either. Probably the typical Roman foods, which you've never tired of. Fragrant prosciutto that melts in your mouth, buffalo mozzarella, figs, tomatoes, fresh dates, smoked scamoza, perfectly seasoned pasta with cream. Finished off, no matter what the exact menu might have been, with cognac; you always had a good bottle within easy reach of your desk.

Afterwards, the group had gone trooping out into the gardens and strolled down the wide path, gravel crunching underfoot. At the fountain of Hermes, B* took her leave. You'd felt a pang of regret, an almost physical torment, with no possible solution, given the present company. You suggested she come for breakfast the next morning (this would pass for a simple gesture of the hospitality due to visitors of the villa) promising her pancakes (in your fridge was a large can of maple syrup brought back from your last trip to NY). Perhaps she wanted to further pursue the conversation you'd started after her lecture. She headed off into the shadows of the loggia to one of the rooms where the Academy houses its guests, speakers, and returning former fellows.

You walked ★★★ to her door and then headed back along the alley of orange trees to your house, isolated in the middle of the gardens. Crossing the main courtyard you glanced at the wing of the villa, counting the windows of the upper floor to see if B★'s room was still lit.

Leaving the gravel path, you slipped between the worn face of a tall bust and the hedge that marked the borders of your section of the gardens.

Seated in your own Balthus painting, you were now contemplating that other, interior painting of your confusion, your turmoil. For it seemed that ever since her talk, an unanticipated attraction had been growing between you and B★. Certainly, you had identified, in the course of the ensuing conversation, intellectual affinities, common trajectories and readings. Nothing is more seductive to you in a woman—you have known this for a while, but it surprises and arouses you just as much each time— than a certain sharp form of intelligence, a manner of bringing that intelligence into play, a freedom of movement in discussion, a self-oblivion in the pursuit of the pleasure of thinking, of understanding. She was inviting you into games of language, and you threw yourself in headfirst.

What did you see in her that attracted you and stirred you so? The contrast of her body, so frail and thin, and a super acute mental intensity. Something limpid in her voice that sprung forth, clear and vivid, from her body. A sensual proclivity for analysis.

What did you have in mind? Pursuing the game you'd scarcely begun. Crossing back through the gardens, bottle of cognac in hand, climbing the staircase leading up to the vertigo-inducing wooden gangway that leads to rooms 16 through 24. Knocking on B★'s door, identifying yourself, proffering the divine bottle and proposing a nightcap. Were you afraid she would refuse? It wasn't a question of pride. Your hesitation stemmed from another concern. For if your offer was accepted, what then? How to proceed from there? You surmised the arrangement of the room's furniture, you tried to deduce the gestures and signs through which B★ would invite you to stay or to leave, to ascend the staircase leading to the mezzanine. In your imagination, all such signs appear as achingly ambiguous, even though you know that, in reality, they seldom are, and that their intended meaning can strike like lightning. But if the temptation is not at all shared, then the threat of seeing the allure of this complicity dissolve, along with the harmonics of meaning that made you desire her in the first place... Was the attraction you had felt in her presence reciprocal? The allure probably had been. Did this precise allure have the same effect on her constitution as it did on yours? She was obviously a woman who liked to seduce, who had lovers. It was impossible to imagine her as prudish, or disapproving of desire in its wild variety.

But would she have a taste for it? And if, out of habit or as a rare exception, she did indulge, what were you getting into? Wasn't your life complicated enough already? Just how far did you want to push polygamy? Your lover in NY, a mistress in Paris, another in this palace. And their suspicions and jealousy were giving you headaches and weighing on your conscience… Did you really need a fourth? Pssh, this could remain just a delicious and perfectly brief adventure. One night, simple and uncomplicated. You kept coming back to it, sketching out this virtual night with B★, and it seemed to you that her body would offer the same delight as her words, that the lovemaking would have the same sensual vigor, the same inventive vitality.

Vertigo seized you as you imagined it, time grew weary as you conjured this vertigo. Then it struck you that you were only imagining, were only letting yourself delve so deeply into your imagination, in order to defer for as long as possible the moment when that deferment would end up ceding the victory to your scruples or to your incertitude, without either a fight or an explicit surrender. Hoping to precipitate a decision, you got up from your armchair and walked back and forth, the bottle of cognac in your hand, from one wall to the other, from the horizon of books to the slant of the staircase. You were imagining too much. Soon, by dint of imagination and meditation, it would be too late to act, to try.

But did you want to try?

You went out into the garden, avoiding the main walk. You took the dirt paths, the least traveled paths, thick with shadow and silence. Strolling in the dark, one can sometimes sense an impalpable veil alight on the face: spider webs spun from hedge to hedge during the night and carried off in passing, webs that stick to the skin, so faint, so imperceptible they're impossible to brush off. Invisible obstacles of devilish and audacious strength, of artfulness and perseverance, and yet so fragile against the tactlessness of a passing body, prey to desire, or a wandering body, prey to incertitude.

[Night 1]

desire preoccupying you. So that her image would be caught in its magnetic field. But no, nothing. Not the least pull of attraction. The gaze and the flesh do not belong, it seems, to the same body: the image of the unknown woman and the pulsing of desire, each the center of different galaxies or parallel universes.

Dance? But dancing will only aggravate this part of you living a life of its own. All the heaviness and tension of desire is concentrated in a wave of mercury whose dull backlash keeps pummeling your solar plexus.

It seemed impossible that, so close to you, close enough to brush against you, C★ did not sense or recognize your body's strange state.

How had this desire managed to creep up on you and catch you by surprise?

A long conversation the previous afternoon, seated on a quay, water beating against a pier. Something in her words that would have moved you, a bared vulnerability... A way to confide in you, breaking with her prior imperious and brusque sentimental demands... As if she was finally abandoning something to your mercy, to your discretion.

A night-time conversation, the day before: a glass of whiskey shared on a terrace overlooking the city; the calm of the night, the weightlessness of the air, the layers of light vacillating all around; the complicity brought on by long silences, solitude, altitude, the distant horizon?

A dance, the night before, in this same nightclub where, since you found yourselves on enemy territory, you had to measure your steps, gestures, and be wary of any furtive contact, and yet, in the distance you both kept, a strange attraction was developing, as if invisible strings or forces linked your two bodies, and without even looking at each other, the movements of the other became perceptible, all the feints to throw her off thwarted, as if her body were prescient or forewarned of your body's rhythm...

A reading you had done together and where it had seemed that she was venturing into you and that she was offering to let you get inside, too. In the sentences, in the breath that carries the phrases, in the voice that pronounces the words, what had she slipped, what charm?

A walk on an afternoon of ruthless sun in the streets of the old town? The cadence of your steps on the dusty ground? The wandering, the meandering, the voice?

After the nightclub, there will be, once again, the walk in the streets, the terrace, the final whiskey, perhaps. How will you resist? You who, in the past, have never even managed to resist far less intense impulses of your unruly senses? Sometimes even neglecting confirmation of said impulses in order to rush to the most discreet of invitations... How we love to exaggerate the power of desire. So resistible, so often. How many times have we truly, savagely, imperatively desired a body? Consider this question, reader, forget your heart's outpourings, your head's effervescence, your surges of vanity: how many times have you felt a desire that struck at your marrow?

It's an enchantment, a bewitchment. Or rather, in all likelihood you will have overestimated the strength of your reason and your will. You believe you are the master of your desires; you think you are free to succumb to them or not; even free to deliberate them.

We screw up, and end up screwing.

To this day, you do not know how, by what means—surreptitious and yet certainly obvious—C★ succeeded in imparting to you this brutal and sad desire which, after flooring you unexpectedly, still appears to you a pure enigma, a singular monstrosity never felt again. You can still see her, voice, face, steps, scent, wandering, a body on which to extinguish this unbearable desire, in which to purge oneself of it, the only way out of vertigo.

C★ possessed the art of the seductress: a nearly infallible intuition of the fault lines through which desire insinuates itself in the other. What had she captured, grasped about you, that gave her such power over your senses for a night? What fracture had her desire diabolically discerned in the architecture of your drives to so subtly pour the potion that dissolves distance, repulsion, defiance, irony, self-possession?

How do these women know?

What kind of Tristan, melancholy and bewitched, do you become, drifting on these waves of Chypre perfume that reach your nostrils, your lips, prevailing over the thick and heavy haze of cigarette smoke you were both drowning in?

Her victory must be acknowledged. You lean over, and in the swaying of bass, the slamming of percussion, the swells of electronic reverb, you whisper your defeat in her ear. Why bother shouting it when she already knows—and probably has for a long time?

[Night 10]

D★

And now for an adventure that, for the longest time, you've wanted to be able to forget, to make it so that it never happened. Every time this story comes back to mind, you wish you had had the intelligence—or the humility—to spare yourself the affair.

There is a chance that tonight's examination of the memories D★ left you and the retrospective glimpse of your own idiocy will irritate you intensely enough to make you give up your project altogether.

Then why choose to give in to it? You certainly have enough stories that are more pleasant, or more interesting, to consider. You're not lacking in material. You have to stick to a contract of thirty nights and not one thousand and one or *mil e tre* (Scheherazade or Leporello? Who can tell the difference?), which would force you to go dig up the most minuscule, the most distant, the most insignificant, the most ephemeral stirrings.

Pluck up a bit of courage, you enjoin yourself, forcing your fingers to transcribe what now appears on the screen. A bit of courage, it's only five awful hours to endure. Perhaps you'll feel better at the end of the operation. If, at least, you could help yourself to a little local anesthesia. But it's not pain that you fear, it's disgust at the bile and the humors that have corrupted these things of the flesh. What do you need? A glass of cognac? Granted.

You write. You pour.

Now, let's calmly consider the question.

It had all begun quite simply, during one of your trips into town when you were living abroad. Trips busy with society life here and that is uniform (for you don't have luxurious or fashionable taste) and heavy-duty (for you only care for what is solid, good quality, what will resist the harsh regime of your habits... all that is light and ephemeral is an immoral squandering in your eyes... if you can't count on these shoes and this leather jacket lasting for ages, what's the point?) and which fills your drawers, stuffs your buffet and hutch, makes your clothing rack buckle, litters your parquet floor, devours your space, and throws a hurdle at each step. And it's a miracle if your mother, visiting you in your exile (for she loves to travel, and is greatly concerned with domestic comfort), has not bought you, out of love, the indispensable cookware and that strict minimum in terms of dish towels, plates, glasses, and silverware without which one lives, according to her, like an animal. Even if it means loading you up like a donkey at moving time... (For how can you throw out a present from your mother? It would be a crime of ingratitude and indifference... No more than the books that you buy, you cannot bring yourself to throw out anything from your mother. Fatal loyalty.) Very fortunate also, if she has not, taking advantage of your absence, surreptitiously left in your kitchen cabinets a preciously preserved part of the inheritance intended for you and which she loads and lavishes upon you by anticipation: a bundle of tea spoons which she carefully explains come directly from some great grandmother (and Lord knows those poor people suffered and toiled to accrue such bequests— the mere thought of it makes you ache all over...), a fragment of your father's trousseau, towels and napkins embroidered with his initials by the nuns of the convent of the old cross-border town, for which he has no use (you didn't know men were given trousseaus; there's a mystery there in need of elucidation; you run to the nearest bookstore, combing through shelves of anthropology, history, and sociology; you discover an extraordinary field of research, questions, speculations; you gather material, you are captivated, you spend a week in your bed between sheets embroidered with the initials of some ancestor—if they don't last for a century, what good are they?—reading volumes; your bed overflows with them... you move to the living room couch...), and then, oh surprise, the first piece of a porcelain set intended as a birthday present (for you have enough books, she thinks...) or even a dozen crystal cognac glasses in case you should have guests over... Guests? Such misery! In what state of enthusiastic delirium were you when you sent out that invitation? You must immediately organize this shambolic mess in which you lie in a state of chronic procrastination... You spend a night sketching bookshelves to house the excess, you regret the absence of a workshop where you could execute this simple woodworking project (you did bring back from the countryside a part of your collection of jointer planes, rabbets, wood chisels, saws, framing squares, and marking gauges, and flew in a crate of English hand planes—all of which now sits enthroned on the mantelpiece, having driven out a few stacks of books—but you didn't have the time to build the workbench of your dreams in your kitchen: your mother and your lover threaten disowning and divorce if you actually undertake the project...).

What to do?

You close this long parenthetical.)

So, you were writing that, when you sum it all up every year, in order to fill out your various tax returns, your expenses, it seems to you that for the past fifteen years you've worked to fatten up bookstores and airlines. And when you met D★, your commuting oscillation from one side of the Atlantic to the other particularly benefited the airline companies. And between two such oscillations, you met her.

Let's say that you remember rather distinctly that she sought to make your acquaintance.

That she had, since you always saw each other in public, the subtlety to indicate to you very discreetly, but very indubitably, her desire. And you'll admit: that alone suffices to stir your desire. Picture a public situation, a soirée, a cocktail party, a meeting, a convention, a dinner, a salon, any congregation in everyday life. Imagine a desire that various proprieties compel you to hide from all those present other than the object of this desire, who feels none initially, a desire that finds no opportunity to declare itself. Calculate the forms and paths of your communication. Measure out the means of your concealment. Find secret strategies of seduction.

It seems to you that this is a dying art. And you still admire D★'s initial sureness in it.

The necessity to deploy such art stemmed from the paradox of this desire's parameters. A social setting, a straight woman, in a society that is also religiously, catholically, jealously straight, and a necessarily clandestine desire for a woman who is not. What codes to play by? What protocols to leverage?

On second thought, a crucial part of your attraction for D★ was tied to precisely that: the secret grasping of signs which, in the middle of a society both blind and supercilious, permitted the initiatory recognition of desire. You both stand amidst a crowd and, from afar, through a phosphorescence of the gaze, of the body, receive the sign addressed to you and perceptible to you alone. You are thereby excepted from the general blindness. Exaltation of a lucidity that seems denied to mere mortals, to mere heterosexuals whose official relaxing of morals (which has not been accompanied by any dismantling of the old privileges and reflexes) has—to hear them complain, as their religion is somewhat comical, oscillating as it does between triumphant dogma and doleful creed—radically disenchanted desire. You are the only ones to see the desire that is not allowed, in what is not said aloud.

You will add two things here. That D* was not the only woman to offer you the vertigo of this esoteric communication of desire. And that, in what the common language persists in designating by the name of homosexuality, the part that always had the strongest pull over your imagination is none other than the semiotics and hermeneutics, so singular, that stem from situations of secrecy that homosexuality may involve. Finally, it's this pleasure of signs that you hold dear above all else, their labyrinth where one hides and captures that which cannot be said (for it is outside the law of normative codes and public languages), that guaranteed you never had the least affinity for the ghetto. There language seems poor, as poor as that of the norm. The radical unknown of desire, the art of its emergence, the strategy of its unveiling have been reduced there to some elementary equations and codified protocols. Rationalization of desire, economic in appearance, you admit, and liberal in its effect. But for the anxious animal that you are (and

Description of a state that could just as well have been idyllic. But, just as narrative fiction is formally indistinguishable from referential narrative (for they mimic each other to such a point that in these twin mirrors only mirages can be glimpsed), the description of pornographic, solipsistic alienation is indistinguishable from that of the perfect shared erotic passion.

So, what's the difference?

The difference is that there was none. D★ had taken a lover and had had the genius to choose a woman to fill the role. But while she might have feared—or met some difficulty with—obtaining a certain something from him, she risked nothing by turning a woman—whom she managed not to notice was one—into the instrument. The relationship thus remained strictly heterosexual.

Such irony would be enough to turn you off of lucidity.

[Night 6]

E★

The image your memory proffers resembles this: a confusedly Gothic conference hall, tables in the shape of a stretched ellipse, your head held in your hands probably to keep it from drifting, and, inside the space where an I resides, a dizzying void resonating with the words of someone from far away, all the way at the other end of that never-ending ellipse. The distress, the intense distress at being condemned to sit there, holding your head. For it will never finish. This feeling you haven't felt since high school. Enduring the surge of endless words, so devoid of passion, so solemn, so full of faith and certitude in what is Good and True. A conclave of true believers babbling and pontificating about a counter-reformation of the articles of literary scripture, post-second coming of the subject.

So you were bored to death at this symposium where, under who knows what pretext, a palette of academics and sundry writers had been gathered. (You would only have to rummage through the shelves of folders that clutter your office and make up the archive of your life to find the symposium program and the text that you read there, but what's the point? You said you would write from memory, and its fault lines are just as intriguing and suited to your project as its peaks.) As a rule, it's not a good idea to line writers up in a room and entice them to talk. It's enough to turn you off of literature (your last line of defense against the fierce disgust the human species tends to evoke in you).

Your boredom must have been obvious; boredom puts you in a bad mood. A French novelist took offense at your words.

At lunch, she sternly reproached you with what she considered to be your outrageously pro-American, dangerously disillusioned, cynically nihilistic opinions. Altogether too many adverbs.

In every debate she tried to contradict you. She had a positive outlook, a great deal of faith, in addition to her adverbs. You are only ever skeptical. The idolatry of literature, its alleged eminent virtues, humanism, hyperbolic worship: they're not for you. Contradiction fortified you; in the abysmal ennui besieging you, it was your only jubilation.

It seemed to you that, far from taking these pointless debates for the banal rhetorical jousts they really were, your novelist took them personally, came to believe you despised her and was hurt. You also had not indicated that you had read her works. You had not demonstrated any consideration. You wanted, on the last evening, to repair the perhaps brutal impression you had made and, asking her for a copy of her latest novel, undertook to read it amidst the brouhaha of aperitif chitchat.

It required you to exhibit a talent that you have acquired through so much reading, which allows you to scan a 200-page volume—provided it's not a grotesque translation of a German treatise on metaphysics—in thirty minutes and retain enough to talk about it. Which you then proceeded to do with the author, competently enough that your remarks and questions surprised and seemed to delight her.

By way of explaining this little talent, this little secret weapon you unveiled, let's say that a novel is like a car: any amateur mechanic knows upon initial inspection the type, its most common pathologies, and the structure of its engine. There are a few common models, a minuscule amount of rare ones that force you to revise your understanding, oblige you to dismantle them completely to understand their workings. We encounter more family sedans on the roads of literature than Ferraris or prototypes. Let's also say that, to your eyes, literature takes after mechanics more so than religion. You see in it neither transcendence nor the ineffable. Rather valves, cylinders, ignitions... Which is to say nothing of the trips it can afford us, nor of the lands it can take us to.

You informed your novelist that her vehicle was well made, its mechanics solid. That, judging by ear, everything ran smoothly, the music of the motor was pleasant, the carburetor well tuned.

The two of you parted after dinner on an excellent note and you went back to your hotel room, planning to pack your bags, for tomorrow the symposium would come to a close, the French novelists would take off for Paris, and you for New York, where you lived at the time. For once, you would go to bed early. How long has it been since you went to bed early?

You stood in your boxer shorts, toothbrush in hand, when the telephone rang. Your novelist proposed that you meet her at the bar for a last drink.

That or insomnia... You slipped on your pants and took the elevator down.

You are sitting at a low, round table in one of those "club" armchairs. Wedged comfortably deep in the chair, legs stretched out before you. The bar is of the red velvet, wood paneling, and softened lights variety. The image in your memory is suffused with its dim red glow. The novelist is named E★, she is sitting to your left in an identical armchair set at a right angle to yours.

battlefield, once more, will be desire. The only question is that of the moment, of the movement, of the event that will begin the battle.

It's three in the morning; you take the elevator. Her room is two floors beneath yours. The door slides on its rails. The corridor is deserted. All that's left to do is say goodnight. You see her hesitate to proffer her hand, leaning, it seems, toward a less formal farewell. Seizing the invitation, you embrace her. It lasts a while. You take the scene in, coldly, though the coldness saddens you. She wrests herself finally, stammers something like, no, I can't. And disappears. You step back into the elevator, press the button for your floor, thinking how it's all so strange and familiar, and a bit tiring, to play this game; to play it again and always according to the standard though implicit rules leaves so little to surprise. Who would dare to invent others? To thwart... Back in your room, you think while undressing that you certainly served literature honorably, these symposiums are decidedly exhausting and you conducted yourself with more tactfulness than you believed was possible, for after all, E* no longer has any reason to blame you—didn't you grant her full satisfaction?

You stood in your boxer shorts, toothbrush in hand, when the telephone rang. One might say it's too good to be true, that your memory is playing tricks on you, reassembling the same shot in the film of that night. Perhaps. But why do you see, so clear and distinct, the blue stripes of the shorts you were wearing?

Here you go again out of your room, taking the elevator back down, threading the maze of hallways toward room number you don't remember what. There is something rather delightful, you think, in journeying thus in the middle of the night, walking past door after door, and knowing that a woman is waiting for you behind one of them. It's a scene out of a very bad novel or a bad film, and the professional mechanic in you relishes it. You'd think it was a parody. And you the willing character. You have taken a seat in a driving school two-cylinder, with two steering wheels, two sets of pedals. The gears shift with terrible scrapings, reverse is barely distinguishable from fourth, the suspension is abominable, and the landscape goes by slowly. The other driver pumps the accelerator and the brakes with both feet at the same time. What a ride.

And before calling you, she has taken a double dose of sleeping pills, or so she tells you…! You're not even sure there'll be enough fuel to reach the next step… She is awaiting, furthermore, an important phone call that she would like to be confidential. You've never seen a driver so terrified of the road she's taken. Has she only ever driven on an uncongested highway, on flat terrain, and with automatic transmission and cruise control on top of it…? Let's engage.

It was as though she was witnessing the spectacle of her own stunned desire. The suspicion even crossed your mind that she was faking it, faking the revving up of the engine, as one does when sitting in a cardboard box and going vroom vroom, pretending to be racing in the 24 Hours of Le Mans.

Her body, naked in the light seeping in through the slightly open curtains, a slender body, tensed up in your hands. Her gaze, fixed on you without pause, without abandon, looms in your memory. It seemed as if she had taken leave of her body and left it in your hands, reacting noticeably but almost automatically to your investigations and proddings. You were tempted to blindfold her, but concluded it would have required compelling her to surrender entirely. To escape her gaze, you lied down on top of her. She instantly wrapped her legs around you, and you buried your face in her hair.

Then you started to get bored. You were tempted almost irresistibly to think of something else. It bewildered you to find yourself sentenced to spend this absurd night in the arms of a mechanical doll whose springs each of your oscillations seemed to wind up, who clung to you but did not move you, and whom you despaired of ever moving. You were freewheeling downhill, and at the intoxicating speed of this ride, the failures of the suspension, far from giving you energy, rattled you. Bad trip. And what idiotic point of honor forbade you from wresting yourself from her arms and ditching her to return to your own bed where you wouldn't be watching yourself neither sleep nor dream?

You know that you fell asleep. But later, filtering through your sleep, a worry woke you with a jolt. That upon opening your eyes, you would see her watching you, see her face leaning over you, spying on your sleep. Insomnia would have been preferable to that.

You asked her what she was doing. She replied that she was watching you sleep. You surreptitiously glanced at your watch. In thirty minutes the two alarms she had set would go off, signaling the agreed upon hour of your departure. Did she remember the deadline that she had so imperatively ordained, had made you promise to respect, and which would signal game over?

You asked her if she was in the habit of watching the people who shared her bed sleep. She said no.

There is a blank in your memory that extends until the moment when she took your hand and brought it against her pubis. You let her position your hand, curious to discover just where she wanted to lead it. More curious still when you saw her close her eyes as soon as she slipped it between her legs. Your fingers sliding along the natural slope, spreading the labia open, you feel her shadowed and palpitating wetness. Her eyelids quiver but remain closed, even when your fingers force their way in and pull back, losing themselves in the folds of her flesh. You listen to her, taking care not to rush her pleasure. Breaking the rhythm when you sense she is getting too close to coming, slipping from one caress to another without leaving her the time to settle in. How strange that she would now let you play her thus, and that her body would follow all the detours you were taking. At what point would she take hold of your hand to force it, compel it to finish, drive it into her flesh and with a thrust of the hips deliver herself from the unbearable elusiveness of pleasure?

But it's the duration imparted to remembrance that, coming to a close, now rushes you to conclude.

The alarm went off. You remember interrupting your unfinished caress. You remember E★'s surprise and reminding her of the promise she had exacted from you. You remember putting your clothes back on, retracing your steps down the still-deserted corridors. Vanished from your memory: what you can't have then helped but think of that night whose constrained coldness, whose paradoxical cruelty and vain anxiety today astonish you.

[Night 3]

does, stringing songs together, remixing the tracks and the phrases of old dramas, old romantic comedies, at the same time.

Later, she gracefully slipped off the stool, thanking you for your hospitality, your conversation, your light, and left blowing you a kiss goodbye and striking a pose of rapture at the foot of your turntables, echoing the first scene of the first act she had performed.

At the end of the night, as the club was closing, the boss asked you what you had thought of her old friend H★. She was lovely. The boss let out a triumphant laugh and in her thick, husky voice of an old madam: You've probably guessed, my dear, he's a tranny. He found you perfectly gallant.

You had indeed suspected: H★'s voice was a little too deep, her femininity too visibly calibrated and calculated. It was, however, unlikely that she had asked the old madam to reveal such information. Why would she? To dispel a blindness from which she would have had little to fear? Why then rat out the secret of an old friend and make confessions that H★ might not have wanted to disclose point-blank to the object of her seductive feints? Petty betrayal, a madam's nasty trick. Triumphal insensitivity that strips off and lays bare in two words the fragile secrets and the painfully composed and guarded modesty.

H★ came back several times to spend the night hours seated immutably on the high stool near you. Smoking patiently, crossing and uncrossing her legs, attracting the looks of the women passing by. There she basked, exposed for all to see, like an obscure object, seductive and fatal, a siren fastened to her chosen rock.

Your manner remained the same. You treated her with all possible consideration. You let her reign over the little kingdom from where you governed the rhythm of the nights. Sometimes she would nonchalantly lean on your shoulder to whisper things in your ear in full sight of all present.

One night H★ told you the story you had been expecting. You had never asked her questions that would have forced her to reveal or disguise the secret of her identity. You had also avoided questions about her vocation, her past and present activities.

Is it really necessary to recount her story in its most tragic or sordid details? I'm probably not telling you anything new. Not of the prostitution, nor of the butchery of these affairs. She seemed to speak of them calmly. And you listened calmly. She recounted just as calmly what had been her biggest fear: that a client, roused from his blindness, in a flash of lucidity or horror, would murder her. Or, alternatively marveling at the fact—was there flirtatious-ness or despair in this remark?—that they never noticed anything, that they did not see the difference, that they did not even see it after she had told them.

She came back to see you once more after this confession. Just as dressed up and lovely as ever. You welcome her as you did the first day—or rather the first night—offering her her usual drink. She takes her pack of cigarettes out from her silk clutch, holding one between her fingers with long, painted nails, which she brings slowly to her mouth lined with a lipstick that's a bit more violent than usual, observing your gaze as it ascends in the wake of the cigarette, from her thighs to her mouth. Deeply inhaling the first drag of her cigarette, lit with the flame of your Zippo. And you chatted about frivolous things, as before, as always; she murmured sundry secrets and nothings in her deep voice.

Then she left, acting out once again at the foot of your cliff the selfsame scene of rapture and regret.

[Night 7]

I

It's three in the morning. You automatically convert that to the time right now on the other side of the Atlantic. You live in two time zones simultaneously (or rather you escape and slip between them constantly). Is it so surprising that you should go to sleep at nine in the morning if it is in fact six hours earlier in another region of your brain? And it's at decent hours that, despite appearances, you get up (except on the days you have to teach… on those days it's torture to wrest yourself from bed at the hour when ordinarily you're just getting into it…). But once rendered on the other side, why are you not free from insomnia?

American night: that's what we call the cinematographic process designed to give the illusion of nocturnal darkness while filming in broad daylight.

It's three in the morning and as you type on your keyboard, your machine pipes into your headphones—for it is actually three in the morning for your neighbors, and thus out of the question to use your stereo—the music of your (real) American nights.

Highway music: something that booms through the speakers, synchronized with the speed of the journey.

Your American life: a road movie without a camera. Average: two thousand miles per month. A record, once, at five thousand miles in three weeks. Highway music, played in a quasi-hypnotic loop on the CD players of the wheels you rent while there. Your rule is to change car every month. However, you have a predilection for certain models. Thus, for a long time, the Pontiac Grand Am (you liked its name: *grande âme* or *grande dame*… for the rest, a decent face, above all dressed in red, but a Spartan drive, ascetic even in its austerity…); if unavailable, Buick Regal or Chevrolet Lumina (soft sofas on wheels… morbid cowards, as you'd say in Italian); finally, sole infidelity, a Toyota Solara. V6 always, coupe as often as possible, and automatic transmission for the fluidity and the cruise control.

It's three in the morning. You're awake. You brew a ristretto. You wedge your computer into your bag. You lock the door. Hit the road. Ahead, five or seven hundred miles to go. You'll drive up or down the East Coast, you'll cross the Appalachians. On a strip of paper you scribble the numbers of the routes you've studied in your Rand McNally.

The streets are deserted. The sky a translucent black. The windows rolled down to let in the scents of the night. The rumbling basslines of your highway music comingle with the rumbles of the V6.

Some tracks are practically glued to the landscapes through which they carried you. They superimpose on the computer screen or the windshield of any car, a strip of road carved up by headlights.

The part of I-95 that, one night when your plane had arrived at three in the morning, takes you north toward New Haven. At the halfway point, you see the power plant plunked down on the estuary of the Housatonic River, drowning at night in the clouds of steam spewing out of all its chimneys. The race against the planes that land or take off from the runways of the Newark airport, parallel to the New Jersey Turnpike, among the giant refineries dotting the swamps, flickering, the only visible stars in a sky smeared by their exhalations. The dim night of devastated

Philadelphia neighborhoods, windows boarded up or gaping, scorched by fire, cadavers of cars embalmed in the tall grass of dead ends. The highway that crosses West Virginia, soaring on stilts above valleys, barely touching the landscape. When it touches it, it's to butcher it. Blasted through the rock, the trenches where your car headlights are devoured. Veins of coal that show on the surface, black, striating the walls. After a mountain pass, a bend, a river. In the cold February night, the tangled volutes of white steam from Marmet's factories, halos of arc lamps illuminating the docks, the barges loaded with an intensely black ore. Ten miles and three bridges later, the gilded dome of the Charleston Capitol. Exiting the Interstate at Ripley to take US-33, the procession of mobile homes and trailers, on each side, American flags fluttering in the wind. At dawn, on the banks of the Ohio River, Pomeroy's main drag looks as through lifted from the photographic archives of the WPA, for at that hour the world is still a black and white picture. A two-lane road—from Michigan, from Illinois?—that no one travels anymore, crosses little towns from another time, solemn when they sleep, heralded from afar by strings of churches planted in open fields. A highway—in Georgia, in Carolina?— a deep asphalt black, lined with reflective strips of a blinding white, in the middle of a never-ending forest. Where you follow no one, pass no one, and discern in your rear-view mirror only the glow of your own sidelights. A lake under the moon, almost Chinese, its flatness defying perspective, gray reeds punctuating the calm silver plane. Your car seems to surf on the surface. Chesapeake Bay swallows up body, lane, and soul. Spiraling ramps and arching suspension cables, a thin strip of steel and concrete surfaces and plunges anew into an endless vertigo. The cliff against which the Tappan Zee Bridge seems to want to throw itself, the elegant swerve of its deck skirting the abyss.

Rrose Sélavy was right: bridges are the great American art.

In the bracing cold of the mountains, in the humid summer heat of the Southern plains, when you stop to get gas, fill up on Coke, and take a leak in the toilets stinking of Lysol, you set foot on the ground, you're walking on the moon. You're two thousand light years away from home. You drive through this place where you will probably never return (there are so, so many gas stations… what are the odds that, even on an identical route, you would stop twice at the same one…?). You stare at the cashier counting your change. When you speak to him, your accent betrays you. You are not from the neighborhood, not from this neighborhood. They'll comment on it sometimes. But can never guess where you're from.

So many miles for what? To feel in the world and outside of the world? In a country that is familiar (you speak the language, you live there) and foreign (you were not born there, possess nothing there but memories without moorings)? You marvel at this land, so vast and so empty.

The fragility of the human presence. These collapsing shacks by the side of Southern roads, windows and doors smashed, kicked in, overgrown with vegetation, a tangle of vines and ivy. In the French countryside, it is said that from one church tower you can always see another. Here, from one steeple, you'll see twelve others in a single file, or else nothing, as far as the eye can see. There are Baptist churches pitched in clearings. And then not even a silo on the horizon. Or else a road lined with gas station, church, motel, church, gas station, church, church, Baptist, Pentecostal, Exxon, Adventist, Best Western, Baptist, Sunoco. A pawnshop for variety. A tattoo parlor for cruelty. For fifty miles. At the sixty-sixth Baptist Church, you decide to take the first right. After one minute, there is nothing but pine forest, cornfields, cotton fields, a mass of undergrowth, the luxuriance of a swamp.

The landscape strikes you as eerie. Not that it's exotic. Nothing really unknown. All of it seen and seen again, in CinemaScope, in real life. Except that it's poles apart from the landscapes you grew up in. Except that it's a landscape you don't know how to photograph. The frame of your car's windshield alone tames it enough for you to take it in. (And that's how you take photos there: at arm's length, in midair, through the lowered window of the right door, or else, surreptitiously, without taking your eyes off the road, straight ahead through the windshield... the camera sometimes aimed at the exterior rear-view mirror...) And just as you will always keep the trace of an accent that, in the depths of Virginia, of Michigan or elsewhere, will betray your foreign-ness, this landscape will always escape your capture: it exceeds the borders of your snapshot, it overflows them. That it's been filmed to the point of blinding the entire world—the images of this landscape have dripped and bled (as we say of a badly fixed color that runs) over the entire planet to the point of inspiring parking lots, shopping centers, and suburban housing tracts all over—will not change anything here. Your gaze, like your tongue, like your culture, was formed in the towns of Europe, in its countrysides and mountainscapes.

The New World is the only truly disorienting one, cutting

across the Old World grain—a full world, of peasants relentlessly tending the land till it's been exhaustively humanized. New World, unoccupied territory, where Chateaubriand thought he had seen shores empty of inhabitants looking at seas empty of ships, and whose hosts, to ward off the anxiety of these infinite spaces they are too few to populate, strive to cover up under sprawling suburbs, distraught metropolises, shopping malls rolled out over acres and acres, a blanket of concrete, parking lots, ramps, bypasses, asphalt. Lay the foundation to cement our disappearance, quickly, for its grip, imminent, threatens. The traces and imprints break down, fade, erased and phantomlike. For having failed to cultivate the landscape they are powerless to possess. America, or the middle of nowhere… This is perhaps the source of the elation that takes hold of you as soon as you set foot on the new continent: in the middle of nowhere, who are you? Here, you are you; there, another; nowhere, no one.

What is so exhilarating about this vanishing of traces, about this ordinary nomad phantomization? And how is it related to the subject that's supposed to be driving these stories?

You were seated at your computer, you had launched the word processing program, plugged your headphones' mini-jack into the back panel, next to the two USB ports, double-clicked on the music player. The clock in the menu bar at the top right of the screen indicated: *Tue 3:07:01 AM*. You didn't know which woman to think about. You told yourself that you could engage any subject, whatever came to mind. What came to your mind was what flowed through the wire connecting you to the machine. Highway music. You embarked upon it. What ought to have been only a primer, a warm-up, became a digression, and the digression stretched for miles (for what path through these nights presents any evidence, any necessity? What path do we chart in the middle of nowhere, at no hour?), taking up the entirety of the ascribed duration.

But how is it related to the subject that's supposed to be driving these stories? And the figure of desire?

The figure is the same and is another. A figure, precisely, and by definition…

That of the Pontiac Grand Am, that *grande dame* or *âme*, American soul that you never stop desiring, object of your most constant desires, reigning over your nights, nights without nights, luminous nights and just as many days. Incomparable flight you never possess, no more than the world it allows you to brush up against, to cut across, so alien and so familiar.

Could you have devised a more beautiful allegory, a more sublime figure of desire?

[Night 11]

K★

You liked the name she called you: kiddo. She took a strange pleasure, perhaps it reassured her, in emphasizing the generational differences between you two, your wild and crazy youth and her maturity of a woman who has lived, who knows what is sensible and what is not— you, for example, and the desire she felt for you.

You hadn't perceived the shift occurring between you from an established friendship to attraction, that madness she fought against, before which she kept erecting obstacles, limits, safeguards.

One autumn night she drove you home, and when it was time for you to get out, she lingered, leaning over her steering wheel, without speaking, without saying goodbye to you, and you waited, puzzled, for her to tell you her secret, a secret you had not imagined. She didn't tell you, but prolonged your hug for an unusual amount of time. Then, after letting go, and before your silent interrogation, added only this: It's ok kiddo.

You got out of the car, confused by that sudden revolution of your shared feelings, asking yourself later, at home, stretched out on the parquet floor of the big empty room that served as your living room, hands crossed under the nape of your neck, if you hadn't dreamt it, and how it was possible that six years of friendship could have, in the space of one night, been converted into a desire you hadn't seen coming. The friendship had probably, from the start, been built on a basis of subtle desire, of a potential desire that good sense, affinity, tenderness had managed to tame, divert, shape into something else.

This desire was worrying you. How would you respond to it?

Were you responsible for it? Had you, by accident, without realizing it, activated or reactivated it? Didn't it threaten your friendship?

The order of what ensued is vague. There is no time in your memory, nothing but places and between them passages that open only to close again. And a meteorological memory, of the texture of the light. Light inseparable from the places and the movement of your body in space, of the vision of other bodies in that space and that light.

There is the halogen light that floods the surface of your desk at the university, the all-nighters you pull working in your office; the light of the computer screen, distinct, surging out of the shadows. The email window turns it to black night streaked with bright green letters. K★ will find these late night messages on her screen in the morning, a few doors farther down the hallway. Emails in which you tell her about your pinball machine feats, your video game triumphs (you spend way too much time in the student game room three floors below), the little hermeneutic discoveries you chance upon in your readings, and then all that one never talks about, for there are things—self, light, meaning—devoid of substance, but whose spectral presence we may try to grasp, to capture obliquely, in fragments, incidental or reflected.

There is the murky, garish light of the video game Mortal K. One night she came to watch you play, struggling against her horror of violence, even virtual violence, which you delighted in, decapitating, blowing up, carbonizing adversary after adversary in an interminable quest for virtual immortality.

There is the incredible light of a late afternoon after a storm that has rinsed the air and rendered a hallucinatory purity to the facades, the trees, all the objects it bathed, leaving behind a pale, bloodless sky, violently intensifying colors, expressing an unbearable darkness from the trunks of trees. You walk through the campus gates, K★ still hesitant, delaying the moment of her response to your plea—let's take a walk?—the coded phrase whereby you had, early on, started signaling the resolution to give yourselves over to pleasure, after a walk that leads you, along the shopping streets, by the old cemetery, through the ghetto, to your house.

You, too, had started calling her kiddo.

It's two in the morning, and you remark that this project you have undertaken, to make an inventory of these moments of your life according to the pure order of desire, is a project that is either insane, vile, or idiotic.

The narration washes up there where you unravel. The autobiographical account is an imposture (as if you didn't know that already): you are unable to unwind the nonexistent spool of a film that was never shot. Fragments of moments superimpose each other, cancel each other out. There are only erasures. In your memory, everything has decomposed and dispersed under the spectrum of what K★ became for you. Could you even render a cubist portrait of her, an allusive portrait, a portrait in fragments? No, not even. Indecipherable. What machine, what fiction must you invent or construct to manage to capture what would only be an abstract figure of K★, a figure pierced with ellipses, and the enigma that you become in the space and light of her memory?

Worse: the desire you both gave into destroyed the friendship—and today, you miss K★. All that she feared from you, from desire and its danger, came to pass. She could not keep herself from feeling it, from yielding to it to the point of inspiring it in you and, having inspired it in you, didn't have the heart to protect herself from it, nor the force not to succumb to it, nor the freedom to abandon herself to it entirely without reservations. You've both left the place where you met. It's been five years since you last saw her. You are dead to each other, and you must resuscitate who you were at her side, and who she was at yours.

You struggle with this impossible memory. You cannot recount K★. Tenderness devastates you. And here is the core of your powerlessness: you had more than desire for her. And when it comes to that, there is no way you can resort to the half-ironic, half-moral perspective that allows for narration. This aloof point of view that outlines and pins down, that immobilizes the memory under the lamp or under the tongue, and, methodically, like a scalpel, observes and describes it. Autopsy. A cold narration, consistent with the coldness of desire.

You cannot recount K★, and the reason is visible in the traces that remain, in that partially electronic correspondence that you keep on a shelf of your library, those gray ashes of phosphorescent signals consumed on the screen of former nights, that you reread a few months ago as one rifles through dust, in search of clues as to the genesis, forgotten like all the rest, of a novel that you conceived of at that time.

In this panic of sudden comprehension, you've just typed a load of nonsense. K★ still remains within all that you are today. There is no one to resuscitate, and it's because the memory is still alive that it resists autopsy and decimation over the course of a story.

You didn't know it then, holding yourself to the comfortable concept of a friendship that had digressed into desire, you still didn't know it at the moment you began writing tonight, but you loved K★, and I suddenly feel with a five-year delay the devastation of having lost a woman that I loved (that you loved?) without ever having known it. And who probably put down all her defenses to love you.

You should have suspected it at the first word written tonight. You should have, in rereading that correspondence a few months ago, understood it all. The dialect in which you wrote to each other is the dialect of all your loves: a chimera of French and English, strewn with bilingual wordplay, vertigos of language, trepidation over meaning. K★ is also, she was already then—that was legible, but how long does it take to understand what one has written without having premeditated it?—the shadow or the double of another woman you loved, who did not look like her, and whom you were still mourning when you loved K★, without knowing it and perhaps without wanting to know it.

Your blindness, so convenient and so well maintained, has just exploded in your face. It's ok kiddo, you would say.

Or is it?

[Night 4]

L★

A gaggle of writers hurtling down the sloping streets of a town foreign to most of them, on the way to a restaurant where they will be fed between two feasts of discourse.

Lost in this cortege, busy chatting *boutique et politique*, was a little girl dragged along, from colloquia to readings to signings, by her stepmother, who was doing a worldwide promotional tour. Putting on a show of her affection.

How old was she? Ten or eleven perhaps. The age of lanky limbs, of a growing body's prolonged clumsiness. The awkward age. Awkwardly dressed by this stepmother. Shoes that did not make it easy for her to negotiate the slopes of the hill our little Parnassus was hurtling down, heedlessly, so much were they absorbed by their *boutique et politique*, paying no attention to the child. She had been celebrated enthusiastically at her arrival, her prettiness and kindness had been praised. The ladies had passed her from arm to arm to kiss her, then came the outpouring of customary compliments to the stepmother.

You went down the street without talking, looking at the river below, straight ahead. And the bank beyond, distant, and the horizon behind, proffered. You see that in your memory: the opening of the space from the point of view of your body pinned to the hillside, gaze delighted by the stretch of world revealing itself far away. You suspect, however, that another perspective has superimposed itself on that image of memory, the perspective you would have perceived on another day, but in an identical light, from the terrace of the hotel where you were staying. Still, the sensation of the air lingers with you, the feeling of an open space, like a kingdom by the sea. You hang over it. You feel as though you could soar over it if you so desired.

The child was close to you, probably because you were the only silent ones. You noticed she was struggling to go down the hill, that the soles of her little girl shoes were sliding on the cobblestone. That, desperately holding back, she was becoming paralyzed. She nearly slipped backwards. You kept her from falling. From that moment on, she didn't let go of your hand.

Sensing that she was still scared, you set about explaining to her how to adjust the balance of her step to the slope, how to relax, to resist, without rushing, the force of gravity that carried her body forward, to identify the vertical and hold herself without fear, using her arms to balance against the momentum of the slope, to set her eyes before her and embrace the landscape to steady her body in space. And to further reassure her, you told her that going back up would be less perilous than going down. That the descent, on mountains, in life, in cities, was always more dangerous than the climb, and that if ever she were to find herself one day on the top of a steep mountain confronting vertigo, all she would have to do is turn her back to the void and go down how she would have climbed, but reversing her steps, facing the slope. Or else, from the side, slanting, in such a manner as to resist the pull of the void and the fall.

This little girl didn't make a lot of noise at the lunches and dinners. She must have been even more insufferably bored than you were. They sent her to bed early, too, as one does. You believe you remember that one evening, as you showed up late for dinner, her stepmother, ★★★, told you that she had been asking about you, had been looking for you, that she had recounted how you had explained to her the art of descending slopes and that she now no longer had any fear because she knew. ★★★ complimented you on your pedagogical talents. You didn't discern any irony in this compliment.

The symposium wrapped up with a brunch where everyone showed up weighed down with their luggage. People moved between tables, swapping seats. You found yourself, not long before the hour of your departure, seated at the same table as ★★★. You chatted *boutique, politique*. You had resigned yourself to it, in order not to appear unsocial.

What you find in your memory when you probe it: there are memory-images that are like paintings defying the articulation of a single perspective. Their focal point is divided between your body as it fits into the remembered space, and the point of view of no one, as if your gaze had become detached from your body. The image of the memory that makes up the painting is thus paradoxically anchored and drifting. These memory-images are rare. You would have needed some sensation to strike your body in order for the memory to fasten itself there: a light, a worry, a numbness, an alarm…

And then, for the rest, for all that did not coalesce into a picture, there is a sort of stenographic scribbling of the past, eliding the repetitions, a sort of partial code, a compressed file, a hasty script, to be completed with all that we know too well, or believe we know too well, the blur of days, of things, of people, of words, of events, of landscapes. And which automatically, or nearly so, comes to supplement the traces, the outlines, following patterns where you suspect our forms, our common habits of narration and description, of playing a part. These are prescribed, taught, indoctrinated by the vulgar and prevailing uses of representation that novels, serials, films, and conversations have forever ingrained in us.

Between the first memory-image that, at the beginning of that night, you considered and attempted to fix on the page... (A sketch, like a study that a painter would have gone to execute in a museum of an inaccessible painting that she can't otherwise obtain, a painting by another painter, that in seeking to copy she can't help but dissect, and onto which she inevitably imposes her own manner... If you can't understand this, go see the copies, the sketches, and the studies that were done over the centuries by all the painters, of paintings of their significant predecessors. In the order of personal memory, too, we succeed each other, aesthetic generation after aesthetic generation. And perhaps the cunning of memory, of fiction, and of life only ever amounts to this: to step into that spectral gallery of pictures we do not remember having painted, but that our senses and time have composed and conserved for us, that another painted for us, and to forever redo our apprenticeship by turning ourselves into copyists—critics, confectioners, kitschifiers, curators, disciples, dissectors, engravers, iconoclasts, restorers, counterfeiters, high priests, translators...) Between the first memory-image and that which at present you will try to summarize, all your narration will have amounted to little beyond the stenographic buzzing laboriously deciphered, decompressed, and transcribed in the common language.

This second memory-image is bathed in an extraordinarily bright light. It comes from the right, entering through what must be the large bay windows of a hotel dining room, intensified still more by the stretch of white tablecloths covering all the tables, perceptible although blurry in the image. Bright light, but you see your body before your eyes like a dark patch (you must have been dressed in black, and the other point of view, that which doubles the place of your gaze set apart from your body, lets you discern, hung on the back of your chair, a leather jacket). The little girl approached silently while you were chatting and stood behind your chair. When the conversation had ebbed back toward the other end of the table, feeling her presence, you turned around to face her. The back of your chair separates you from her. Her face is level with yours.

She has placed her forearm or her hand on your shoulder, as if to dance. The memory is of silence and stillness, of the weight of this child's arm on your left shoulder, of her sad eyes fixed on yours, of an infinite duration. But you also know that she spoke to you. You also know that behind your head, where the table is, where the light is coming from, also comes an ugly wave of whisperings and looks that you can't see but that tug at your gaze, which you strive not to turn away from the child who is speaking to you, so seriously, with a determination interspersed with silences, without seeming to pay attention to that which you do not see, behind your head, but that she can't avoid encompassing in her field of vision.

The child asks you timidly if she will see you again, if when you come to Paris she will see you, if you come there often, if New York is far. A cloud of wickedness envelops you both, saturating your perception. You strain not to turn your face away from the child and confront the gaze that you feel on your back, make it stop by dissolving that strange colloquium with the child. To not turn around. To listen to her, respond to her, pay her the necessary attention, possess her calm and patience.

When the child with the sad eyes will have let her arm slip from your shoulder after having gravely said goodbye to you and will have gone off as silently as she came, you will face the table once again. ★★★, with a little smile, a bittersweet voice, then offered out loud her interpretation of the scene. She had apparently not missed a word and meant to expose its meaning. Obviously, she said, you represented for the child, because of the ambiguity of your appearance, the figure of prince charming promised to little girls by fairy tales and whom at this age, unconsciously, etc. The girl awaited prince charming and had mistaken you—grotesque error—for him. ★★★ had therefore seen very precisely, under the pretext of Perrault and Freud—or rather of Walt Disney and Bettelheim, those two counterfeiters—what she had wanted to see. And you had seen her see it; you had felt her drooling gaze on your back.

You shrugged your shoulders, refraining from making any comment. If, by some fluke, the story was indeed a fairy tale (for ★★★ might have been mistaken about the genre of the story itself, rather than the child about your gender), in ★★★'s version, the stepmother, i.e. the witch, an obscene narcissist, a jealous caster of spells, transforming everyone she kisses into toads, had absconded. With her apple poisoned by the tree of tactless, lawless, and falsified knowledge.

[Night 5]

N★

That year, three factions made up the preparatory classes at the Lycée Henri IV: the studious commoners, a priesthood of political fanatics, and a decadent and libertine minority.

It was ten years before the revolution of '89.

The studious commoners would sit on the left side of the classroom, closest to the windows, just beneath the professorial gaze; the libertines on the right side; the militant clergy, for their part, strategically wedged between these two wings.

You were not of a fanatical disposition, nor of a laborious one. For the first time in your life, you could finally do what you wanted. Done with the ten hours of math and the nine hours of physics that had been inflicted on you weekly for years on end by the wisdom of your parents and their legitimate ambition for you. You would never attend X nor Centrale nor any other school of the kind. You certainly wouldn't have gotten in: the entrance exam requires a masochistic diligence whose secret you do not possess, or a passion that the academic machine is rarely capable of arousing.

Since you had early on started indulging the vice of solitary reading, you had eyes only for what one no longer dares to call the humanities. (And it's a shame, you think sometimes these days, that in your assignments you didn't encounter books that would have been able to inspire in you an analogous passion for the sciences. When you glimpsed, a few years ago, at your junior and senior year math books before putting them away on the highest shelf of your newly built library, you were seized with anger for the pedants who had had the nerve to inflict such abominable puke on generations of unfortunate students. You had forgotten that the point of this instruction was never to instill an affinity for the subject but to make it into a pure instrument of selection. It would be pointless, thenceforth, to call on native intelligence or curiosity to offer the least adventure, the tiniest escapade. We could—and what a scandal it would be—discover a passion for mathematics; who knows where that could really lead us, and society swept along too. You had to reach thirty and read English fluently in order to delve into an honest history of mathematics and finally learn something of it. Literature, though minutely minced and grotesquely drowned in the aseptic brew of Lagarde and Michard, was still surfacing in scraps.

Culture on that side, although crumbling, boiled down, was not yet fully attenuated and neutralized. The vaccine wasn't perfect. A paragraph of Montesquieu, of Stendhal, or of Flaubert, a verse of Baudelaire, of Aubigné, or of Racine, even amputated, disfigured, coated in bland commentary, could still prove virulent on a susceptible constitution. You fear that the latest pedagogical improvements have eliminated the last remaining chances of accidental inoculation.)

But you digress. Yes, you could have developed a passion for mathematics but you only had eyes for the disciplines of meaning and interpretation. You had reached, at last, their blessed land. Glorious emancipation. Literary libertinism was no longer a hidden vice cultivated in secret.

You could indulge your other inclination too in such a liberal place. Quite a year you had there, happily filled with all kinds of darings and temptations, of free pursuits and affairs.

You will tell the story of one among many. Why this one rather than another? So be it.

You will tell a few others, too, another day, soon. They have the charm of coming-of-age novels. Does it not seem to you, twenty years later, that everything then, even your passions, your feelings, had an energy, an optimism that has since been lost? Delightful illusion conjured up by the retrospective narration of youth: wasn't the world newer then, and your sensitivity, too?

Charming topos. Young imbecile that you were, trusting in her own strengths, filled with wonder at the thought of trying her young powers in intellectual disputes, in exhilarating projects of seduction. You were finally, you thought, in your element. To prevail in rhetorical exercises, to overcome all rivals at intoxicating speed. To learn, know, and conquer everything through the free play of the mind.

One, then. Why her? Because, young imbecile, your adventure with her had the same effect on you as your scholarly trophies. A triumph of will, a price for excellence snatched in a fierce struggle in the ferocious competition of libertinism.

N★ was by all possible accounts a very beautiful woman. Everyone, even the austere priesthood, longed for her. A knockout. You've since been told that she made the cover of a magazine dedicated to the exhibition of female nudity.

You feel a pang of regret. You knew so little of her in the end. The only portrait you would be capable of giving today is all exterior. A portrait on glazed paper offering only an icon for fantasies. And on the verso, the features of a beautiful intelligence… And yet—but how can you express this, how can you capture this in the fragments of memories still accessible to you, she was something other than that… Confusingly, you feel it, you know it, even though her figure lacks density, as if ghostly…

You don't even know anymore how it all began, through what maneuver you had convinced her to go on a date with you. Through what little note borne from seatmate to seatmate up to her desk. For a real polyphonic epistolary novel was being composed during class in the rows of the right side. A concentrate of *Liaisons Dangereuses*, bastardized with German metaphysics.

Writing this title, the memory of the circumstances, uncannily, comes back to you. There I go. You were lavishing your epistolary attentions on ★★★, who, still hesitating to give in to your entreaties and, perhaps to buy herself some time, or to complicate the affair, suggested, or enjoined (you no longer remember), that you pursue the conquest of N★. Was that the condition of her consent to your wishes? (Perhaps, for not longer after, she did in fact yield to your desires.) She even offered to intercede between you and N★. N★ had made it known to her that she was curious about you, perhaps that she was interested in you, and maybe more. It's possible that even though in your young vanity you believed you had won over N★, it was she who had subtly brought you to precisely the position she had calculated. (You believed you were laying systematic siege to a fortress, maundering about the battlefield…)

You no longer know what ★★★ wrote to her (perhaps you never knew), nor what you conveyed to N★.

In any event, it was a Friday, the day before some vacation (Easter, you think). After lunch you strolled with N★ through the streets of the Latin Quarter. You still remember the men doing a double take as the two of you walked by, those who whistled and your stupefaction at such a spectacle. Your indignation. If you were her (but obviously, you are not her), you wouldn't have put up with such a barrage of scurrility, you wouldn't stop yourself from slapping their moronic mugs once and for all. Obviously, you are not accustomed to causing riots in the streets. You still aren't accustomed, either, to being thrown out of a café by a waiter, more jealous than scandalized by your alleged indecent behavior, which happens nearly right away when you have spent a few moments kissing on the bench of the dark back room of a bar near Odéon. Precise memory, here, magnificently precise, of the obstacle of N★'s barely-ajar teeth pressed playfully against your tongue.

It was out of the question to go cause a riot in the Jardin du Luxembourg. Cafés were not a good idea. This exclusion was also new for N★. Normally, she tells you, she has no problem. You bring to her attention the small difference between this and the norm. (Specify, for the intelligibility of the story, that at the time your hair had been quite long.) Finally she proposed that you go to her place, close to Saint-Sulpice, provided you let her check first that there's no one home.

You remember waiting for her at the foot of the building, deciphering the titles of old books on the stand of a second-hand bookseller, in a state of mortal terror mixed with excitement, for you had never imagined that the adventure would go so far so fast. You had anticipated some flirting, but now the possibility of a room, a bed, was looming. And how would you act? A Stendhalian panic was flowing through your limbs. Not a single book title made sense, and N★ still hadn't come back. Perhaps she was retreating too, maybe the building had another exit and she had slipped away while you were consulting abstruse volumes of yesteryear to kill time, to kill the wait. The suspicion, crossing your mind, pricked your vanity and your pride at once. Mortified impatience, excited panic… Wayward head and heart.

But she came back.

In the kitchen, on a table, near a bird cage sitting on newsprint, there was a chessboard, a game already started.

In the bedroom, a piano.

And then what? It didn't help quash your panic to tell yourself that the entire world would certainly have liked to be in your place. It also didn't help vanquish your paralysis to whip up your pride and envision the exercise as a test on a competitive exam where the point was not only to do well but to excel, to prevail over the entire world. And what was the difference between that and a challenging essay question?

Then what? Here's when the indefinite that eludes your memory comes back to haunt you. Then, there was N★, who probably, unlike the young imbecile that you were, had more sensuality and tenderness than vanity, and probably, in not taking you for the entire world, saved you despite yourself from your infernal pride and wretched libertinage.

You decipher retrospectively, outlined in negative space, all that you are unable to say or describe of N★. Something of her subtlety, her quality. Which today you can neither say nor describe for, young imbecile that you were, you did not perceive it, even if it fortunately affected you as N★, in her great gentleness (for that afternoon spent in her bed, everything was gentle and subtle), bestowed its grace on you.

You're reminded of that comic scene of the *Confessions* when, in the arms of the superb Venetian courtesan whose name, you believe, begins with a Z (like the name, you suddenly think, of the obscure object of desire of a Balzacian novella), Jean-Jacques, in the throes of a delirious panic, suddenly loses his composure. And Z★, saddened and hurt, pronounces a sentence which N★ mercifully spared you: *Giacomo, lascia le donne, e studia la matematica.*

[Night 8]

retrospectively betrayed the feeling that had led to a confession so hyperbolic (but perhaps the hyperbole should be attributed to the narrator and not to the character of that incredible story) and so public, in a car full of strangers. It was comical: you were the last person to know, and by accident, about the desire you had sparked.

You didn't think about it again until the moment, two or three days later, when you were getting dressed to go to the gym. You always put on your gi in your office, thus shielding your modesty from the lack of privacy in the dressing rooms. You also liked to walk like that, in your uniform, under the trees of the campus. It allowed you to inhabit the place in a certain manner, rather than simply crossing it like one is condemned to pass through French universities, for example. You understood that night, stripping off your clothing and putting on your uniform, that this ritual also served the purpose of giving you the time for your metamorphosis from a professor who solemnly receives students during office hours into a student ready to indulge in hand-to-hand sparring. Knotting your belt, you thought again of the unknown woman who, despite your metamorphosis, always perceived the professor and the frog under the uniform of the student. And, walking under the trees, you promised yourself that you would pay strict attention tonight to all of your gestures and try, without betraying anything on your part, to detect the desire beneath the unknown woman's uniform.

This self-defense class was very interesting indeed. Students fought under the direction of a remarkable sensei: a short, not skinny, black woman born and raised in the Bronx, living in the Bronx, black belt in jiu-jitsu, and marvelously capable of inspiring combativeness and courage in the most timid of the young, well brought-up girls who made up a good part of the class.

Green haven of friendly feminism and pragmatic methods: there you would dissect all the situations of aggression one might encounter, whether the target be your purse, your virtue, or your life. Analyze them, invent ways to block them. Simulate the confrontation if it was the only feasible strategy. In turns, each woman played the victim or the aggressor. The hand-to-hand was firm but thoughtful and careful. So much so that at the end of the semester, to have her class confront more muscular situations and less considerate adversaries, the sensei invited the university's football team to come act as the aggressors.

So that's what you did three times per week. And after ★★★ had blurted out the incredible story, you went to train with an added trepidation and a redoubled consciousness. Each woman who approached you (for partners were rotated to vary weights, tactics, and morphologies) to offer herself as a victim to your acts of violence or as a perpetrator, you saw as an adversary, a partner, but also as the possible unknown woman who perhaps would be betrayed by a gesture that was a bit too emphatic or a bit too soft. You gained a sharp, unprecedented consciousness of the weight of bodies, the proximity of faces, the pressure of hands, of limbs, of their abandon to your efforts, of their resistance.

In your quest to discern, to guess which amongst these bodies was inhabited with desire for you, all their gestures, movements, contacts were eroticized. You assaulted these successive bodies with tenderness, you offered yourself to their endeavors with curiosity. You went to class as one goes on a date. A sensation of physical lightness, the prospect of vertigo. And yet, neither your suspicion nor your vague desire ever managed to fasten onto any one body. The unknown woman did not give herself away. Or else, if you thought you discerned a sign, just as soon you were seized with doubt: in the state of erotic exaltation you were thrown into, who could testify to the validity of your interpretations? If one woman, aiming to grab hold of your head and slam your face against the tatami, had incredibly gently suspended the gesture, holding your skull firmly and cautiously before dealing it the fatal thrust, didn't another woman later on, while you tried your hardest to bear down on her with all your weight, didn't she, before turning you over like a pancake and pummeling you with frightening strikes that stopped, suspended, precisely a centimeter above your sternum or your pubis, didn't she dither and dally, prolonging your embrace?

You never discovered who the unknown woman was. No declaration of her desire was ever addressed to you. No certain sign. You are grateful to her for that. The mystery of her identity, the search for signs, the hermeneutic passion it inspired in you, made that semester of self-defense the most arousing erotic experience of your life. An eroticism that was all the more strange since it never managed to fasten itself or settle on any one body, but instead was bound to all of them, and because it was fluid, vacillating, drove you to pay to each of them an intense and infinite attention. The exercise, a delicate and secret asceticism to guess the enigmatic desire of the other, utterly enchanted the body. Your own, all of yours.

[Night 2]

Y★

Your first interview seemed different from all the others you had in the same circumstances, for the same purpose.

You were young and still believed, on the verge of one of your careers, that you had ambition. You never set your heart on the pursuit of these careers. They proceed haphazardly. You certainly work—at university, at writing—but the necessary sociability with your peers, with the arbiters of your destinies—university types, literary types—bores you out of your mind, and you avoid it as best you can.

Y★, for her part, was on the road to becoming what she now is: revered, feared, and hated all at once, as a power in the field where those prized careers play out. All that, for her as for you, was still to come. Her passion was palpable in her words. She had traveled, lived elsewhere (which in your milieu was the exception rather than the rule).

Your tastes seemed similar; your attitude with regard to your tastes even more so.

You imagined that this first feeling of closeness, of complicity, could only deepen with time. Desire wasn't far off. You got into the habit of thinking of her as a friend.

Friendship seems to you today the most difficult thing in the world. You attempt it, and almost always doubt its reality. Thus the turn to desire, we resort to it, believing it will give form and flesh, the tangible weight of certainty, to phantoms and chimeras and through desire we dispel them, imperceptibly.

You had always known her to fall for strange affairs that seemed to captivate her entirely, distant and absorbed at the same time.

She was then the lover of ★★★ who, years later, would confide in you that her fears regarding her dominion over Y★ had revolved at the time around two rivals, you and another—who indeed became the chosen one, the happy recipient of Y★'s affection and confidence.

It was as if ★★★ had lifted a veil before your eyes.

You had never seen things from that angle, that of rivalry, of conquest, of dominion. You had even lacked the ability to imagine things from such a perspective. (Did you know that the society in which you were (sometimes) living was still a court society? And that the Ancien Régime had never ended? Multiplied, displaced and diffracted, it reigned more supremely than ever.) There would have had to have been someone to show you the way, the goal. There would have had to have been someone exerting enough power over your imagination to lead it onto the path. Curious aporia… You would have needed the spiritual direction of an Abbot Herrera to point out for you the steep road of worldly ambition and deception.

And even then…

Your reading of the human comedy is quite queer. Sensitive, certainly, to the pleasure of intrigues, to the fantasies of power, to the mechanics of rivalries and jockeying for the upper hand, you fail, nevertheless, to identify and project yourself: mimesis, even wishing and willing to succumb to its power, does not inspire in you the desires of a Rastignac. Looking at the spectacle of this world, you can't help but recognize, here there and everywhere, swarming around, the puppets of Balzacian passions. Politics, literature, management overflow with them. There is no career in all of Paris that was not ghostwritten by the creatures of the Comedy.

We have an abundance of young youngsters and old youngsters of both sexes, ambitious, as naïve as they are cunning, in thrall to their own little *bildungsroman*. Channeling (often without knowing or else knowing too well) *Corteggiano*, apocryphal instructions of a baroque cardinal of yore.

What will then have prevented you from emulating the heroes of this society's canonical plots? The text says splendors and miseries of courtesans, and lost illusions…

It also says *femme-écran*…

The funniest thing about it is that a lot of people around you have a clear-sighted view of the plot. If they did not outline it for you (or is it that you failed to recognize and decipher the hints they possibly dropped?), it's clearly because they thought you were already aware of its necessity and its obviousness. Did they believe that you would naturally be inclined to pursue it, as they would have, had they been in your position, since such inclination is supposed to come naturally (thanks to a thorough inculcation in the great narrations of said society) to all ambitious subjects.

These spectators probably still consider you an imbecile today, and certainly secretly despise you for having wasted the opportunity, and for having failed to jump into an affair so promising and so obvious. Had you discerned it, would you have been able to throw yourself into it? For want of cynicism, would you even have had enough bad faith to delude yourself that such a conquest could form the natural extension of a beautiful friendship and not of a vulgar affair?

But aren't you exaggerating your pessimism here? Was your affection for Y★ doomed to corruption? Couldn't it have escaped the fate and faults of the milieu that had borne it? Wasn't there a margin, an outside, a haven to shield it from the inquisitions, the constraints, the vanities?

In that sphere of desire, can there ever be a love story without a plot? We cannot lead a worldly life without getting caught in the web, trapped in the weave of its design. And when we think we have radically managed to escape it—in the frenzy of desire—it resurrects its laws, its comedy, its control. Our desires are over-blown—theatrically and vulgarly: dictated and stolen.

And so for a few years you have been suffering strangely upon recognizing the signs of the possession of the other.

Would you have wanted to be for Y★ what the other was for her, whom she seems to desire? Will you ever know? For you do not know what he is to her. At best you might discern what she is to him. Power is without mystery. But in what then does Y★ indulge?

You suffer perhaps because this specter of power has been emptied of its promise—the bond you imagined between you and Y★— or perhaps all it has done is reveal its vanity. It feels as though you are entertaining a friendship with a ghost or a shadow of her. When you start doubting the reality of your feelings and fear having only dreamed or fantasized this ghost out of thin air, you reread a book that she wrote long ago, when you first met. And each time people mock in front of you this or that position that Y★ has taken or favored, which so obviously betrays the influence of the other, you can't help but defend her even though this position turns you off.

Isn't it only natural that our acquaintances, in cafés, in town, in bed, end up influencing our views, our opinions? Judgments are not at all reflections, but made to accommodate those of the circle of our acquaitances. Our habits prompt our judgments more than our tastes do. Can one shed them without tearing apart the circle of friendship? And how can we tell a taste from a habit, an inclination from a subjection?

At the same time, you feel a sort of sadness, for the imposture is obscene and cruel, and disfigures Y★, whom you love and didn't know how to protect (or perhaps conquer...).

You are resigned, however, and are sometimes mad at yourself for the idiotic sentimentality of your attitude. It is, after all, completely ridiculous to still feel the force of a bond that is always refuted and thwarted by the rarity and superficiality of your exchanges... But that is further complicated, for, beyond and beneath the frivolity and the professional chitchat you exchange, she sometimes happens to tell you things that are curiously intimate. And you don't know how to interpret these moments or these confidences. You feel (or do you imagine?) something else, perhaps something real (what an absurd hypothesis...). Are these the moments when her guard is down, the moments when the former persona of Y★ surges from under the hard armor of frivolities, strategies, and courtship rituals? Or else are they also inauthentic, another ruse or habit, a ritual behavior, a tactic of these milieus: the affectation of profundity, the exhibition of a sincerity destined to reassure us, all of us, that we are still very human and not the grotesque automata of a stock plot? Is it simply that the private, the intimate, the things felt are only extra ammunition for a war game of frivolity? And how should you respond, to what should you address yourself: to the ostensible appearance, or to the furtively discovered depth? Must you show that you glimpse something that troubles you, show that you recognize something perceptible, that you're ready to understand it and protect it like a secret? Or must you, just like her, repudiate it, enjoy it, not insist, and remain in the realm of social levity? Is it out of prudishness that she acts thus? For to insist would perhaps reveal or expose some vulnerability...

But we have learned that this world is traitorous and that the surest way to preserve what we cherish is to devalue it overtly so that no one would think to take it, to flaunt it so that no one can expose it for what it is or steal it.

Defiling what is sacred to us so as not to be taken hostage...

Or else indecency stretches so far into the intimate because everything is profane, because there is no secret, no interiority, because everything can be put to use for schemes, control, subjection...?

Thus we have that paradoxical and concomitant overestimation and depreciation of desire, intimated in the language we use to speak of our erotic lives... In terms manifesting its vulgarization, and in the tone and accent we use to pronounce them, pretending we will not be imposed upon by the power of the thing. Hygienic, necessary, metronomic: the driving score, with no syncopation or breath, of a municipal fanfare or a spin dryer. That banality blown out of proportion; that showcased insignificance... You suspect that the sort of lexical volunteerism used by your interlocutors is the fruit of an effort, of a concerted resistance to an intimate sentiment that it would be too ridiculous or childish to expose. And it seems to you that, through an additional act of ruse or resistance, the shameless assertion which would seem to be merely paradoxical prudishness—or better, just as much prudishness as shamelessness—is beyond our control and runs without stopping, the prudishness dictating the shamelessness that unveils the prudishness, the one signifying the other and canceling it out in the same utterance; familiar strangeness, through which the shameless assertion preserves or calls to renounce the possibility of its double, of its other—defends itself from rendering its secret to Eros, its inestimable poverty offered as a sacrifice to the ostentatious abundance of our consumer mores.

Ultimately, you act as if the thing were real and felt, and as if you were still speaking with the woman you believed you knew. You realize, after the fact, the absurdity of your conduct and sometimes fear that she will interpret your response as a sort of affected sentimentality, the marks of affection as weakness or calculation. And at the end of it all, you are still surprised by the distant marks of her benevolence toward you, and ask yourself if it's the ancient bond that perhaps never was, or was only fleetingly, that faithfully dictates them, or else something else (but what? You are tired of rereading Balzac, Gracian, Acceto, La Rochefoucauld...). And still, you ask yourself now and then why you see her so seldomly. Is it because she finds you so remote, your interests perhaps too distant from the world that haunts her, this world that absorbs her, it seems, entirely (this world where she absorbs herself entirely? to flee? to surrender herself? or else because there is no other...), or if it's because she feels as awkward with you as you have felt for a long time with her, uncertain as you both are of the plane on which you might meet, the virtual or the artificial, and afraid to choose one or the other. And above all, does this all take place only in your head, where not even the phantom limbs of a brief dead past reside, only the pure hallucinations of meaning, the psychological moiré effect without a shred of substance, the shadows without bodies to carry them, nothing but you and you playing against yourself—are you not your best adversary?—at the ancient and unreasonable game of analysis.

And all that, all your interminable dissection of shadows, is still too psychological and naïve.

A little cynical and banal splinter pricks you during your mental odysseys, instilling in the Jansenist and contemplative animal the suspicion that the world is nothing but a battlefield splayed with interests, fights, and strategic ruses of ambition and power, inauthentic through and through, authenticity being nothing but the ultimate fiction deployed by the inauthentic to better help you delude yourself, and what you believe to be moral delicacy or an inner and sovereign leaning is only the function (or screen) of your powerlessness to pursue the only truly real things that exist, here and now, that you don't have the virtue to desire without scruple, for you lack the courage to recognize that there is nothing in this life (the only one we will ever be given) beyond influence, vanity, women, fortune… But is it your fault if you lack faith? If you don't manage to believe in these objects, if none enchants you? All that you have experienced of them, when you still believed you desired them, never gave you any pleasure. The whole religion of subjectivity (the idolatry of desires, the logic of diversion, the theosophy of rivalries, the art of subjection) seems to you grotesque. All that appears to others solid and pleasurable turns to smoke before your eyes. If it had sufficed to get down on our knees to believe… Ironic aporia of sovereignty: Mustn't we get down on our knees to ascend to the throne?

Sometimes you miss Y*.

One morning, in a taxi that was taking you toward an airport, a train station, a lecture hall, the radio tuned in to some cultural program brought you her voice, the naked, enchanting voice of Y* that it seemed you had never heard before in its nudity, in its harmonics, in its inflections, her specter, the erotic fulguration of a desire without history and without hope.

You think of how simple it would be to call her, meeting her in some discreet garden, a dark café. Perhaps the figure of what you desired would appear: to ravish her in her milieu, as if it were possible to strip her of these traits that she was probably driven to adopt in order to adapt to this world and the sort of Darwinian competition it compels. Irony: this heroic desire of stripping exceeds control itself, absolutizes it. More irony: in terms of milieu, you don't have one, you've developed no specific adaptation to any and that's what makes it so that you are thoroughly not at home anywhere and that these phrases are the only milieu that the two of you will ever share.

How to unknot the thread of desire. Dream up nights. Wander again among the shadows.

[Night 9]

Z*

She had accompanied you to the airport. Your memory is saturated with airports, with goodbyes in terminals. You had had a last coffee together before separating, seated face to face, on either side of a table studded with circular stains left by the bottoms of glasses of previous travelers and, bringing your two coffees, the waiter wipes it down with his damp and dirty rag. She says to you that it had been spotted this morning while she was getting out of the shower, on her left shoulder blade, a strange and dark scar she had not managed to glimpse with her own eyes, no matter the effort she made to grasp at an image through a game of surreptitious reflections—even skewed—of her back in the mirrors decorating the bathroom. She says she remained silent and settled for wrapping herself up in her towel. She also says that she had wanted to ask you what this scar looked like, the one that escaped her gaze, her ruses, but she is afraid the scar will cause confusion, that she will be asked where it came from.

She says she was afraid that questions would be asked; perhaps she had even hoped so, this mark on her back asking for it. She is haunted by the question she was expecting but that was not asked.

The travelers got up, they were called to board their flight, they left their small change rolling on the table among the dirty cups and saucers. You asked her, perhaps brusquely, if she was angry with you for having left that scar on her shoulder. You tried to imagine it. You would have liked for her to show you. You can't ask her to undress in the middle of an airport. And so for her to describe it to you, but she did not see it, she cannot glimpse it, to give you an idea.

She feels it like a dull burning in her back, or else a hole in her skin, opening onto nothing, with neither bottom nor edge. When you think about it, it probably looks like all the imprints teeth leave in living flesh. A taste of blood rushes to your mouth and she must have seen your jaw tense up remembering the bite. Looking at you then, did the desire that had made her beg you to inflict this pain in the middle of pleasure come back to her?

Later, you accompanied her back to the parking lot. She had planned to leave you at the end of a long hallway leading to the escalators. That's where she would tell you to go back to the departure lounges. Through the big glass walls you can see the clouds rushing from the edges of the horizon, darkening the sky. You watch the first drops of rain fall, you see them make the first concentric waves, the first disturbances in the puddles of water abandoned by the last showers.

While you stroll together, you suddenly urge her to imagine your plane crashing: the scar that she wants to disappear, out of fear that it betray her, and you also, that scar, how it will become dear to her when the one who imprinted it on her skin will have died... The planes taking off deafen your words. You tell her again to imagine, day after day knowing it will vanish, night after night more pale in the mirror veiled by a mourning kept secret, the memory of you fading at last from her body and this palimpsest sign that she alone—who cannot see it—and you alone—who will no longer be—would have known how to decipher, will become a dead letter. But planes don't crash, you hear her respond. Only sometimes, less often than cars crash... And if she were to die on the way back in an accident, the imprint of that inflicted bite would

blend indistinctly with the wounds disfiguring her flesh, the amo-
rous pain of your teeth on her skin would be lost in the confusion
of blood and warped metal where no one would be able to read…

It was time to separate. You had left many times before, and many
times she had accompanied you to this airport or another, but that
had been before. Before the imposition of this stigma on her body.

You remember having stopped at the foot of the stairs to hold
her back and tell her that all this could be a story in a novel
recounting two lovers at the moment of departure, in an airport,
at a crossroads, at the gates of a city, at the drawbridge of a castle,
somewhere, in an attempt to cheat their suffering. In the novel,
you say, they would separate at the top of a flight of stairs, the
plane would crash, would disappear over the ocean, lost at sea far
from any beacons… And she, would she recall, would she have
recalled, the fiction that you would have told her, of the lover and
the scar that made her renounce remorse, the secret posthumous
symbol of pleasure?

[Night 12]

POST SCRIPTUM

And of course, you were in-fucking-capable of abiding by the rules you set for yourself at the start of this project. It's no longer even a clinamen, it's maximal deflection…

Did you really think you could lead what is referred to as a regular life and stick to metronomic typing in the sober morning hours? For as long as you held back from giving in to your inclination, which has always been to write at night, your project remained in limbo. It probably would be more honest (although insignificant) to change the title to Not One Night. But that would violate in its turn the rule whereby you decided to eschew second-guessing and crossing out, and to make it so that what was written is unwritten. So it goes, from one transgression to another, until we have eviscerated the entire body of laws…

As for writing every day or even every night, that was rather optimistic… Did you really bank on so easily curing yourself of your cardinal vice—procrastination? It didn't even take a week for you to grow bored of yourself. Sufficient unto the day is the woman thereof? Hardly. There are so many books that you haven't yet read, that you're tempted to flip through… Writing and women will have to wait a little while longer yet… Chateaubriand kept you up until the small hours, and the mornings that you had dedicated to your writing task found you in bed with a man who died more than one hundred and fifty years ago. You should have engaged in writing orgies to make up for time lost from going to bed so late so that you can in good faith say you have never stopped going to bed early. You would have had to double down and simulate several nights in the space of a single one. You certainly tried, but that didn't last either... You are possibly no longer fickle enough for such debauchery. Chalk it up to human weakness...

Better: you abandoned your project for months on end. Uncertainty contending with acedia. The danger was over. These writings, left incomplete after they failed to fulfill their purpose in a timely manner, come back to haunt you sometimes. What good would it be to pursue them? There were nights still, when, unsure whether to execute the program, you buckled down to the chore. What should have been a month's work was disseminated over more than a year.

And as for writing simple sentences... Pious vow. Even speaking, you can't manage it. You touch on an idea and bam! You can't help glimpsing a vast landscape of detours and reliefs that you allow your sentences the pleasure of wrapping themselves around, threading their perspectives and winding according to their meanderings.

To top off the measure of your unreliablity, beyond the promises (but was it promises that the ante scriptum made? Predictions, announcements, engagements? And who did they bind? In breaking them, what were you perpetrating? An imposture, a crime, a swindle?) that you didn't keep, the constraints you diverted, the contracts (subject to what jurisdiction? Made with whom? Yourself? A reader, silent, who isn't even a person, at best the signifier of one, and admittedly, less than a signature? Quid of their consent? It will be deemed to have been tacitly granted... These contracts of writing and reading are a quasi-legal fiction upon which are founded our most serious uses of discourse...) that you broke unilaterally, not to mention the clauses you kept secret?

One in particular, which should suffice to send the entire construct teetering: in the series of nights, there is one, at least one, that is a fiction. And you won't tell which.

Look for the fiction.

A most delightful twist, it came to you at the start. For if one of these exercises of memory is fake, and no one knows which, how is one to read them? The status and the interpretation of each are indefinitely suspended; the approach of the entire series is uncertain. How will you henceforth (re)read them, reader? As fables or as true stories? And what lesson shall you draw on the nature of desires exemplified within them?

But it's a twist whose deliberation compelled you to think twice. How would you construct such a fiction?

Would it suffice for you to reread and examine the sequences of authentic recalling to identify their turns and to be able then to replicate their form and movement? Old method to gain credence. Wouldn't too sharp a reproduction betray your own hand? The imitation might veer off into pastiche. It could also happen that this section might end up resembling each of the others, none alike, in a kind of family resemblance.

You could also turn to the chimera and stitch back together fragments of memory of different origins. Give to your creature the desire of one, the body of another, the voice of a third.

Mixing the places, the times, superimposing the faces, cutting out the qualities and the vices. Smoothing the whole, splice by splice, to rig out an apparently seamless fable.

You could also, since your memory is equally made up of cultural and literary figures, instead of letting the telling reveal the emblem that gives the key (as in musical notation rather than locks) of such an exercise of memory, you could elect one among the many common places of the rhetoric of desire and to this figure entrust the direction and the substance of your story.

After which, it all comes down to inventing the incidental qualities required to clothe and cloak that find. Leave it then to some carefully balanced combination of method and chance. Method, for chance practically never crops up unalloyed in stories. Generating randomness exceeds the forces of the human mind: it takes machines. The animal exudes sense and determination like it pisses, like it speaks, like it breathes. Irrepressible rhythm… How easily one falls into step… Chance, for method betrays itself through too much consistency, too much saturation, and the excess of signification leaves the suspicion of premeditation from which one must protect oneself if one wants to be believed and exonerated on account of one's naïveté.

But do we really know, between improbable coincidence and implacable consistency, which one signals and betrays fiction?

In any event, prudence called for crafting fiction out of these diverse methods, mixing their means and their strategies: impurity would be your principle.

There remained, once the cycle of these exercises had more or less been carried out (lingering well below the number you had set, these thirty days or nights, for really, once the reason that had driven you became null and void, what did it matter that there were thirty nights or thirteen or twenty-one? Since the point had been to go against your ideal of literature, against your aesthetic ambition of the integrally calculated work, why not let oneself be led by pleasure, or one's absence of pleasure, to continue, to start up again, to advance...), there remained the most delicate question to deliberate: What to do with this little heap of sentences? Was it really reasonable to imagine publishing them?

If you were to publish these exercises, didn't you risk, no matter the precautions, hurting such or such a person who would recognize herself—rightly or wrongly—under some initial?

Hadn't you taken care that these stories be abstract enough to prevent a positive identification of their subjects? You even pushed precaution to the point of scrambling the initials designating them. That was simple: put in the chronological order of their event in your life, these memories offered you a sequence of letters to which you applied a very classical cryptographic method. (Thus, their reference, though kept secret, is no less objective. To encrypt is not at all, in the first place, to feign; quite the opposite, isn't the cipher strategically destined to insure the authenticity—as much as the secret—of the message?) Then, doesn't the clause you used to throw fictional suspicion on each of your stories seal the indetermination of them all?

Finally, if such or such a person, formally recognizes herself under one or another initial and in this ink-mirror does not find her reflection flattering, wouldn't she have herself to blame for having had the curiosity to read a book published under your name, in which she knew she ran the risk of encountering herself? Will she accuse the book or her desire to see herself figured in it, and find herself there, bared, even though forewarned… And to those who might object to the memory you have kept of them, you will respond that this memory stems from you just as much as from them: why didn't they leave you a nicer one? But that is very much hypothetical. You don't think you have really mistreated the characters of your memories. And as for those you did mistreat, who can say that they didn't deserve it…?

[P.P.S.:] One of my close readers remarked to me: Quid of those who will not find themselves in these nights? Doesn't omission risk hurting, too? My only excuse in this case—if it is to be dragged out—would be to invoke my laziness, its vagrant rovings through my memory.]

Wouldn't you hurt, moreover, your own modesty and, by extension, that of those close to you (is modesty ever an individual thing?) by recounting what, with reason, morality used to demand (for, in a perfect reversal, the mores of our time tirelessly enjoin us to unveil, to disclose: cunning of morality, more subtle still than that of reason, as it dons the mask of its own subversion, just as in an earlier age it pretended to disapprove of what it furtively called to the light) that we hide or at least not publish?

Easy to parry. You'll remember to tell your loved ones to stay away from this book. It's a book that you intend only for your adversaries, or else for strangers. And if one or the other of your close friends or kin gives you grief over your unexpected turn to the confessional, you will remind them how often they remarked that today's readers demand entertainment, less philosophy and more boudoir than you usually give them. They kept insisting that in order to achieve success (a legitimate ambition of theirs), you must abide by the style of the day, no matter how corrupt. Which, to the extent of your talent and your proclivities (mostly contrarian…), you have tried to do.

Weren't you in danger, as you strove to skirt the era's idolatry of desire, of being perceived of worshipping at the same altar? With any publication, misunderstanding (carefully cultivated and sanctioned) is the rule of the day. It might be used against you to fold you back into the flock.

To be sure, since your book belongs to the genre classically known as confessional, and strives to achieve an anatomy of desire, why would any reviewer hesitate to lump you together with that orgy of pen pushers devoutly pimping their own asses? Idolizers, fetishists, pornographers occupy the terrain, build chapels, totems. But is that any reason to cede them the entire continent of desire? Just because so many of your contemporaries have colonized the territory should you, for fear of being caught in such vulgar company, in such a bad zone, avoid it, and so yield to an ultramodern, radical, and spectacular form of censorship? (But perhaps the take-over and paving of the expanse of desire is already completed… carved out in subdivisions, devoured by the housing projects, rabbit cages, and shopping malls of the libido… Your fatal attraction to the literary conceit…)

Worse still, and don't recoil from the possibility: what if, thinking you are resisting the pull of the dominant discourse, you were in fact practicing that very French form of resistance we call collaboration?

That is the most worrying of all. Are you not succumbing to a subtle and formidable deceit? A bit analogous to that old paradox inherent to the claim that non-being is not: the denial ironically posits the very suspicion of substance it attempts to erase… But that may be giving too much credit (gilding with metaphysics) to the pathetic little speculations of the pornocracy that this era secretes as naturally as the State secretes bureaucracy and society, in all sincerity, secretes hypocrisy. But who's to say that your critique of desire isn't just another tool of its empire? Are you not, unwittingly, spreading the propaganda, like an epidemic infecting every corner of our post-modern Western world, just as those who denounce its evils enhance the idol's aura?

Can we escape from the publicity of desire? (And what do you mean by that?)

Some people still feel outraged that no car, no detergent, no commodity, no good, no object sells without advertising—which is the art of indoctrinating the multitudes into the ritual of desire (we have billboards and ads as others have muezzins, once had stained-glass windows or hymns, so that the articles we might otherwise fail to fathom might sink into our consciousness and might supplement our poor grasp of our needs and duties, for we are unable to desire the goods without a prompt, an instruction, or a particular grace)—decking it out in its frills and fetishes. Is the point really to sell you something, tempting you to acquire a good? Does it not seem to you that the commodity is a pretext for indignation, for speculation... Advertising sells one thing and only one thing. Do you truly believe it refers to a world of commodities?

Wrong.

All it talks about is itself and its wellspring: desire, pure.

Thus the legions of naked women on their knees, the orgy of spectacular bodies paraded on walls, screens, pages... You still believe that the origin and secret of surplus value, the dangerous supplement, stems from labor? You're still the same old vulgar Marxists you always were... The transcendental horizon of value and its base is desire. Besides, who's still saying you have to work? But to desire, still and always, to keep desiring, endlessly, full throttle, running on empty, in mourning, on your deathbed, amidst massacres, at the foot of a gallows, whatever...

They'll break you in, my friend.

By way of bodies, stripped, available, offered, provoked. By way of pornography lavishly broadcast and piped through every existing network and media and those still to come. By the vindication of transgression, subversion and their rigorous discipline. By way of hysterical release of all these old Victorian, Puritan hang-ups which, for too long, and too painfully, blocked all of you...

And the high priests will keep cantillating that Thou shalt not retreat from thy desire.

And the great Chamberlain will keep swearing by their great

gods that there will be no shortage of fuel or spare parts for our desiring machines.

And the great Inquisitors, after having subjected all parties to the ordinary and extraordinary question, will keep insinuating—which is to say liberally decreeing and pronouncing—that some princess from a novel of dubious canonical status, who preferred a rest to the object of her desire, god forbid, was damned by masochistic and narcissistic neurosis...

And the mendicant orders will keep decrying the distributive injustices, the scandal of good fortunes and erotic privileges, and selling nostalgia for a primitive time when desire was purer, when the deregulation of the elementary structures of the traffic in bodies had not yet debased the chaste fraternity of cum.

And the blissful will keep burning incense at the monstrance of the mystical *objet petit a*, maintaining rigorous accounts of their daily devotions, of every last kneeling. They will loudly profess not having once in a quarter century been visited in the middle of the most severe orgies by perverse pleasure, so ardently were they spurred on by hope in the promised ecstasy, the ineffable Assumption.

For coming, you shall come, in truth you were told, it has been promised, provided you carry on fervently celebrating the holy office of desire.

For coming, our economy, our human commerce, the very possibility of our religion demands it.

For coming, in kind, cash, or credit (credit above all, to the point of usury), you shall come, that is contractually stipulated in the new pact.

You will get laid and it will be paradise on earth (but how is that different from the old credo that says you will get laid to rest and it will be paradise in the heavens?).

What could we object to in such a universal religion? The torments of doubt, the falterings of impotence, a flaunting of anticlericalism… none of this, nor heresy, moreover, nor any schismatic move, will ever carry any consequence. It's the least that the empire of desire can expect from its subjects, the very condition of their sincere worship.

Incredulity alone is sinful.

Thus, in the minor orders known amongst the clerics as literature, henceforth the only recognized vows shall be what the subject confesses publicly as the grateful expression of pure desire: a poetics that shall be a liturgy or an orgy, and a litorgic or liturgiastic oeuvre.

Irony alone is damning.

The flesh will be bland and you will believe you are forever reading the same book.

Thus draws to a necessary close, at the end of the five hours devoted to writing according to a rule that you instituted sixteen months ago (and the only one that you scrupulously enforced), the last nocturnal excursus of this little volume composed at the margins of memory, according to an art which is memory's own, and at the whim of your good pleasure.

[On Apple Macintosh machines, July 19th 2000–November 19th 2001]

Restraint can be generative. An Oulipian writer, Anne Garréta is accustomed to writing within restraints: her debut novel *Sphinx* is a love story written without identifying the main characters' gender. But *Not One Day*, though given parameters, is not an Oulipian book. It doesn't follow its own set of rules. Garréta opens with the intention of writing five hours per day, each day for one month, and each time recollecting one woman she's desired or who has desired her. She'll write them in the order in which they come to her, she says. She won't alter them after they're written. At the end of the month, she'll put them in the alphabetical order of their initials. The book will be a "stammering alphabet of desire"—will locate, spell out, delineate it in Garréta's life.

But in the end, we discover this has not been the case. We've been misled: we understood her story as one language, and now we learn that she's been speaking a different language. Instead of an alphabet, the sections of the book have delivered us a story from beginning to end, in chronological order. Furthermore, Garréta broke off writing the book for months and then returned to it. She has forfeited every rule she set out in the beginning.

Do we now go back and read the book again, to reinterpret the meaning of its events? Except, Garréta tells us that one of the sections has been fictionalized, and she won't say which, nor will she give us the clues we would need to figure it out. Her true desire cannot be located within the text. As she says about the possibility of knowing an author through her novels: "no subject ever expresses herself in any narration."

Though *Not One Day* is a work of nonfiction, it is nonetheless a collection of constructed narratives. As a story, it's limited to the semiotics and hermeneutics of storytelling: language, culture, action, and time. Though these stories originated in Garréta's own life, and we feel the emotional labor of her writing them—where five hours a day seems manageable at first, later it feels like all that one can bear—as the author she remains at a certain remove from her recollections, observing and interpreting the subtext of her characters' dialogue, their gesture. She compares them to the invisible threads of a spiderweb, delicate but strong, ensnaring, more felt than seen. With the nightly designation at the end of each section, indicating when Garréta recollected it, we're reminded of the interlacing neural pathways that hold these memories.

One way that Garréta brings awareness to the construction of the narrative is in her use of the second-person point of view. In the second person, Garréta sets herself apart from herself, can coldly observe her own behavior—she also becomes the object of her own desire. She addresses herself, and directly addresses the reader, making the reader another desired object—and the reader reciprocates. The text itself becomes interrelational; there is a back-and-forth movement, dialogue—someone giving, someone receiving—ever-shifting victim and aggressor, desirer and desired. The use of "you" creates a focal point, even as it slips away—allows us to track its movements, follow it. Otherwise, desire would be all over, too diffuse to be detected.

Even as Garréta observes herself as a character, she observes herself as an author. Her "you" turns scolding at times, such as when she gets off-task—at other times, it is fascinated with itself, such as when she observes a tendency of her own memory: "What you find in your memory when you probe it: there are memory-images that are like paintings defying the articulation of a single perspective." Even in this sentence, the focus of the "you" slips again: Does she intend to use the collective "you", or is she talking to herself, or talking to the reader? Like a subtle gesture passed between desirer and desired, its meaning could be multiple.

Not One Day performs desire. It is tempted away from predictable courses, the "common narratives." Garréta regularly takes long digressions from the present story to muse on seemingly unrelated topics such as mathematics, or her tendency to overspend on books and travel. She's uncomfortable with her experience of desire at times: its messiness, its vulgarity. She prefers the more serious, more rational diversions of the mind in philosophy and literature—and distrusts the "libertinage" of confessional literature, writers writing about their own lives. But she's also tender, and in observing desire's behavior in her life, she comes to understand it. It won't be contained or restrained. It won't follow the rules you set out for it. It is the opposite of reason, and yet it is the universal religion and "transcendental horizon of value and its base." Like light and sound it is ever-present. Its only rule is to desire more of itself.

Sarah Gerard

ANNE F. GARRÉTA is the first member of the Oulipo to be born after the founding of the Oulipo. A *normalienne* (graduate of France's prestigious École normale supérieure) and lecturer at the University of Rennes II since 1995, Garréta was co-opted into the Oulipo in April 2000. She also teaches at Duke University as a Research Professor of Literature and Romance Studies. Her first novel, *Sphinx*, hailed by critics in France and the US alike, tells a love story between two people without giving any indication of grammatical gender for the narrator or the narrator's love interest. She met Oulipian Jacques Roubaud in Vienna in 1993, and was invited to present her work at an Oulipo seminar in March 1994 and again in May 2000, which led to her joining the Oulipo. She won France's prestigious Prix Médicis in 2002 for this novel, *Not One Day*, awarded each year to an author whose "fame does not yet match their talent" (she is the second Oulipian to win the award; Georges Perec won in 1978).

EMMA RAMADAN is a translator living in Providence, RI, where she is co-owner of Riffraff bookstore and bar. She is the recipient of a Fulbright grant, an NEA Translation Fellowship, and a PEN/Heim Translation Fund grant. Her translation of Anne Garreta's *Sphinx*, published by Deep Vellum, was nominated for both the PEN Translation Prize and the Best Translated Book Award. Her recent translations include Anne Parian's *Monospace* (La Presse), Oulipian Frédéric Forte's *33 Flat Sonnets* (Mindmade Books), and Fouad Laroui's Prix Goncourt-winning story collection *The Curious Case of Dassoukine's Trousers* (Deep Vellum). Her forthcoming translations with Deep Vellum include Laroui's debut novel in English *The Tribulations of the Last Sijilmassi*, and Brice Matthieussent's *Revenge of the Translator*.

Thank you all for your support. We do this for you, and could not do it without you.

DEAR READERS,

Deep Vellum Publishing is a 501c3 nonprofit literary arts organization founded in 2013 with a threefold mission: to publish international literature in English translation; to foster the art and craft of translation; and to build a more vibrant book culture in Dallas and beyond. We are dedicated to broadening cultural connections across the English-reading world by connecting readers, in new and creative ways, with the work of international authors. We strive for diversity in publishing authors from various languages, viewpoints, genders, sexual orientations, countries, continents, and literary styles, whose works provide lasting cultural value and build bridges with foreign cultures while expanding our understanding of how the world thinks, feels, and experiences the human condition.

Operating as a nonprofit means that we rely on the generosity of tax-deductible donations from individual donors, cultural organizations, government institutions, and foundations. Your donations provide the basis of our operational budget as we seek out and publish exciting literary works from around the globe and build a vibrant and active literary arts community both locally and within the global society. Deep Vellum offers multiple donor levels, including LIGA DE ORO ($5,000+) and LIGA DEL SICLO ($1,000+). Donors at various levels receive personalized benefits for their donations, including books and Deep Vellum merchandise, invitations to special events, and recognition in each book and on our website.

In addition to donations, we rely on subscriptions from readers like you to provide an invaluable ongoing investment in Deep Vellum that demonstrates a commitment to our editorial vision and mission. Subscribers are the bedrock of our support as we grow the readership for these amazing works of literature from every corner of the world. The investment our subscribers make allows us to demonstrate to potential donors and bookstores alike the support and demand for Deep Vellum's literature across a broad readership and gives us the ability to grow our mission in ever-new, ever-innovative ways.

In partnership with our sister company and bookstore, Deep Vellum Books, located in the historic cultural district of Deep Ellum in central Dallas, we organize and host literary programming such as author readings, translator workshops, creative writing classes, spoken word performances, and interdisciplinary arts events for writers, translators, and artists from across the globe. Our goal is to enrich and connect the world through the power of the written and spoken word, and we have been recognized for our efforts by being named one of the "Five Small Presses Changing the Face of the Industry" by *Flavorwire* and honored as Dallas's Best Publisher by *D Magazine*.

If you would like to get involved with Deep Vellum as a donor, subscriber, or volunteer, please contact us at deepvellum.org. We would love to hear from you.

Thank you all. Enjoy reading.
Will Evans Founder & Publisher Deep Vellum Publishing

LIGA DE ORO ($5,000+)

Anonymous (2)

LIGA DEL SIGLO ($1,000+)

Allred Capital Management
Ben & Sharon Fountain
David Tomlinson & Kathryn Berry
Judy Pollock
Life in Deep Ellum
Loretta Siciliano
Lori Feathers
Mary Ann Thompson-Frenk
& Joshua Frenk
Matthew Rittmayer
Meriwether Evans
Pixel and Texel
Nick Storch
Social Venture Partners Dallas
Stephen Bullock

DONORS

Adam Rekerdres
Alan Shockley
Amrit Dhir
Anonymous (4)
Andrew Yorke
Anthony Messenger
Bob Appel
Bob & Katherine Penn
Brandon Childress
Brandon Kennedy
Caitlin Baker
Caroline Casey
Charles Dee Mitchell

Charley Mitcherson
Cheryl Thompson
Christie Tull
CS Maynard
Cullen Schaar
Daniel J. Hale
Deborah Johnson
Dori Boone-Costantino
Ed Nawotka
Elizabeth Gillette
Rev. Elizabeth
    & Neil Moseley
Ester & Matt Harrison

Farley Houston
Garth Hallberg
Grace Kenney
Greg McConeghy
Jeff Waxman
JJ Italiano
Justin Childress
Kay Cattarulla
Kelly Falconer
Lea Courington
Leigh Ann Pike
Linda Nell Evans
Lissa Dunlay

Marian Schwartz
& Reid Minot
Mark Haber
Mary Cline
Maynard Thomson
Michael Reklis
Mike Kaminsky
Mokhtar Ramadan
Nikki & Dennis Gibson

Olga Kislova
Patrick Kukucka
Patrick Kutcher
Richard Meyer
Sherry Perry
Steve Bullock
Suejean Kim
Susan Carp
Susan Ernst

Stephen Harding
Symphonic Source
Theater Jones
Thomas DiPiero
Tim Perttula
Tony Thomson

SUBSCRIBERS

Ali Bolcakan
Amanda Harvey
Amanda Watson
Anita Tarar
Anthony Brown
Ben Fountain
Ben Nichols
Ben Nichols
Blair Bullock
Chris Sweet
Christie Tull
Christine Gettings
Courtney Sheedy
David Christensen
David Travis
David Weinberger
Elaine Corwin
Farley Houston
Frank Garrett

Ghassan Fergiani
Horatiu Matei
James Tierney
Jeanne Milazzo
Jeffrey Collins
Jeremy Strick
Joe Milazzo
Joel Garza
John Edgar
John O'Neill
John Winkelman
Heath & Martina Dollar
Kimberly Alexander
Kristin Porter
Lesley Conzelman
Margaret Terwey
Marta Habet
Martha Gifford
Matthew Lovitt

Michael Elliott
Michael Norton
Neal Chuang
Nhan Ho
Nicola Molinaro
Patrick Shirak
Peter McCambridge
Rainer Schulte
Steven Kornajcik
Suzanne Fischer
Tim Kindseth
Tim Looney
Todd Jailer
Tony Messenger
Tracy Shapley
Whitney Leader-Picone

AVAILABLE NOW FROM DEEP VELLUM

MICHÈLE AUDIN · *One Hundred Twenty-One Days*
translated by Christiana Hills · FRANCE

CARMEN BOULLOSA · *Texas: The Great Theft* · *Before* · *Heavens on Earth*
translated by Samantha Schnee · Peter Bush · Shelby Vincent · MEXICO

LEILA S. CHUDORI · *Home*
translated by John H. McGlynn · INDONESIA

ANANDA DEVI · *Eve Out of Her Ruins*
translated by Jeffrey Zuckerman · MAURITIUS

ALISA GANIEVA · *The Mountain and the Wall*
translated by Carol Apollonio · RUSSIA

ANNE GARRÉTA · *Sphinx* · *Not One Day*
translated by Emma Ramadan · FRANCE

JÓN GNARR · *The Indian* · *The Pirate* · *The Outlaw*
translated by Lytton Smith · ICELAND

NOEMI JAFFE · *What are the Blind Men Dreaming?*
translated by Julia Sanches & Ellen Elias-Bursac · BRAZIL

CLAUDIA SALAZAR JIMÉNEZ · *Blood of the Dawn*
translated by Elizabeth Bryer · PERU

JOSEFINE KLOUGART · *Of Darkness*
translated by Martin Aitken · DENMARK

YANICK LAHENS · *Moonbath*
translated by Emily Gogolak · HAITI

JUNG YOUNG MOON · *Vaseline Buddha*
translated by Yewon Jung · SOUTH KOREA

FOUAD LAROUI · *The Curious Case of Dassoukine's Trousers*
translated by Emma Ramadan · MOROCCO

LINA MERUANE · *Seeing Red*
translated by Megan McDowell · CHILE

FISTON MWANZA MUJILA · *Tram 83*
translated by Roland Glasser · DEMOCRATIC REPUBLIC OF CONGO

ILJA LEONARD PFEIJFFER · *La Superba*
translated by Michele Hutchison · NETHERLANDS

RICARDO PIGLIA · *Target in the Night*
translated by Sergio Waisman · ARGENTINA

SERGIO PITOL · *The Art of Flight* · *The Journey* · *The Magician of Vienna*
translated by George Henson · MEXICO

EDUARDO RABASA · *A Zero-Sum Game*
translated by Christina MacSweeney · MEXICO

MIKHAIL SHISHKIN · *Calligraphy Lesson: The Collected Stories*
translated by Marian Schwartz, Leo Shtutin,
Mariya Bashkatova, Sylvia Maizell · RUSSIA

BAE SUAH · *Recitation*
translated by Deborah Smith · SOUTH KOREA

JUAN RULFO · *The Golden Cockerel & Other Writings*
translated by Douglas J. Weatherford · MEXICO

SERHIY ZHADAN · *Voroshilovgrad*
translated by Reilly Costigan-Humes & Isaac Stackhouse Wheeler · UKRAINE

FORTHCOMING FROM DEEP VELLUM

EDUARDO BERTI · *The Imagined Land*
translated by Charlotte Coombe · ARGENTINA

ALISA GANIEVA · *Bride & Groom*
translated by Carol Apollonio · RUSSIA

FOUAD LAROUI · *The Tribulations of the Last Sjilmassi*
translated by Emma Ramadan · MOROCCO

MARIA GABRIELA LLANSOL · *The Geography of Rebels Trilogy: The Book of
Communities; The Remaining Life; In the House of July & August*
translated by Audrey Young · PORTUGAL

PABLO MARTÍN SÁNCHEZ · *The Anarchist Who Shared My Name*
translated by Jeff Diteman · SPAIN

BRICE MATTHIEUSSENT · *Revenge of the Translator*
translated by Emma Ramadan · FRANCE

SERGIO PITOL · *Mephisto's Waltz: Selected Short Stories*
translated by George Henson · MEXICO

SERGIO PITOL · *Carnival Triptych: The Love Parade; Taming the Divine Heron;
Married Life*
translated by George Henson · MEXICO

ÓFEIGUR SIGURÐSSON · *Öræfi: The Wasteland*
translated by Lytton Smith · ICELAND